The REZ DOCTOR

GITZ CRAZYBOY • VERONIKA BARINOVA
AZBY WHITECALF • TOBEN RACICOT

HIGHWATER
PRESS

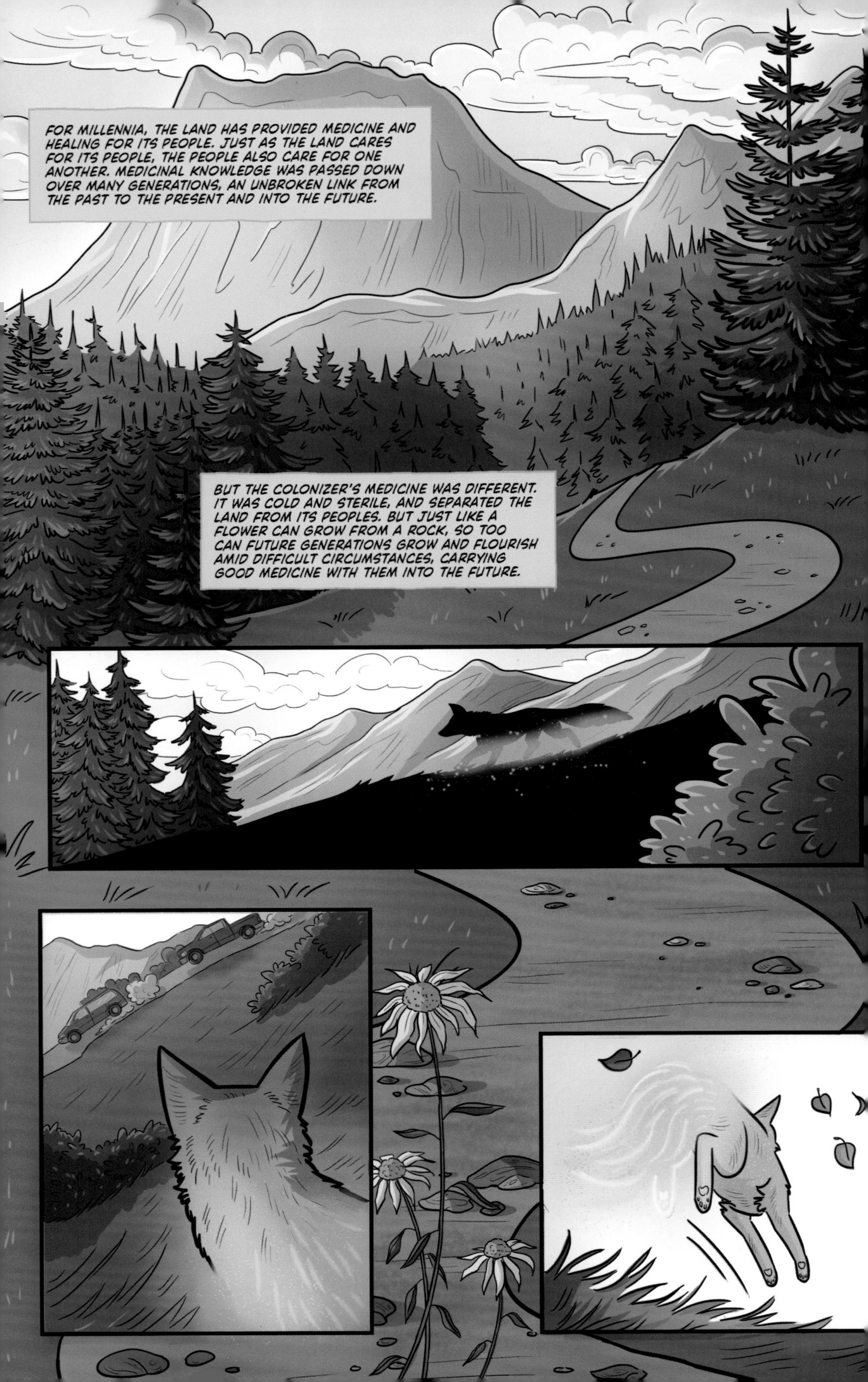
FOR MILLENNIA, THE LAND HAS PROVIDED MEDICINE AND HEALING FOR ITS PEOPLE. JUST AS THE LAND CARES FOR ITS PEOPLE, THE PEOPLE ALSO CARE FOR ONE ANOTHER. MEDICINAL KNOWLEDGE WAS PASSED DOWN OVER MANY GENERATIONS, AN UNBROKEN LINK FROM THE PAST TO THE PRESENT AND INTO THE FUTURE.
BUT THE COLONIZER'S MEDICINE WAS DIFFERENT. IT WAS COLD AND STERILE, AND SEPARATED THE LAND FROM ITS PEOPLES. BUT JUST LIKE A FLOWER CAN GROW FROM A ROCK, SO TOO CAN FUTURE GENERATIONS GROW AND FLOURISH AMID DIFFICULT CIRCUMSTANCES, CARRYING GOOD MEDICINE WITH THEM INTO THE FUTURE.

Kainai First Nations.
Mid-2010s.

TRIBAL CLINIC

WALK-INS
WELCOME

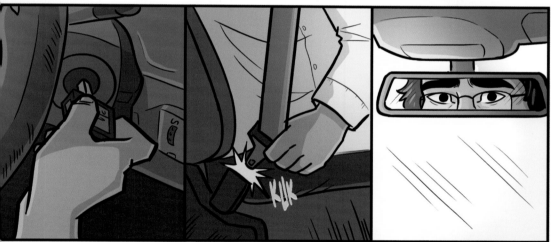

KLIK

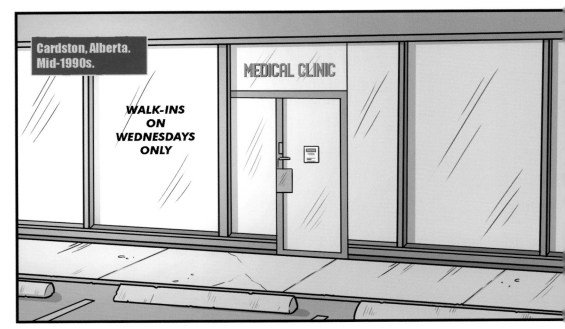

MEDICAL CLINIC

WALK-INS ON WEDNESDAYS ONLY

Wash Your Hands!

I DON'T NEED PAINKILLERS--I NEED *HELP!*

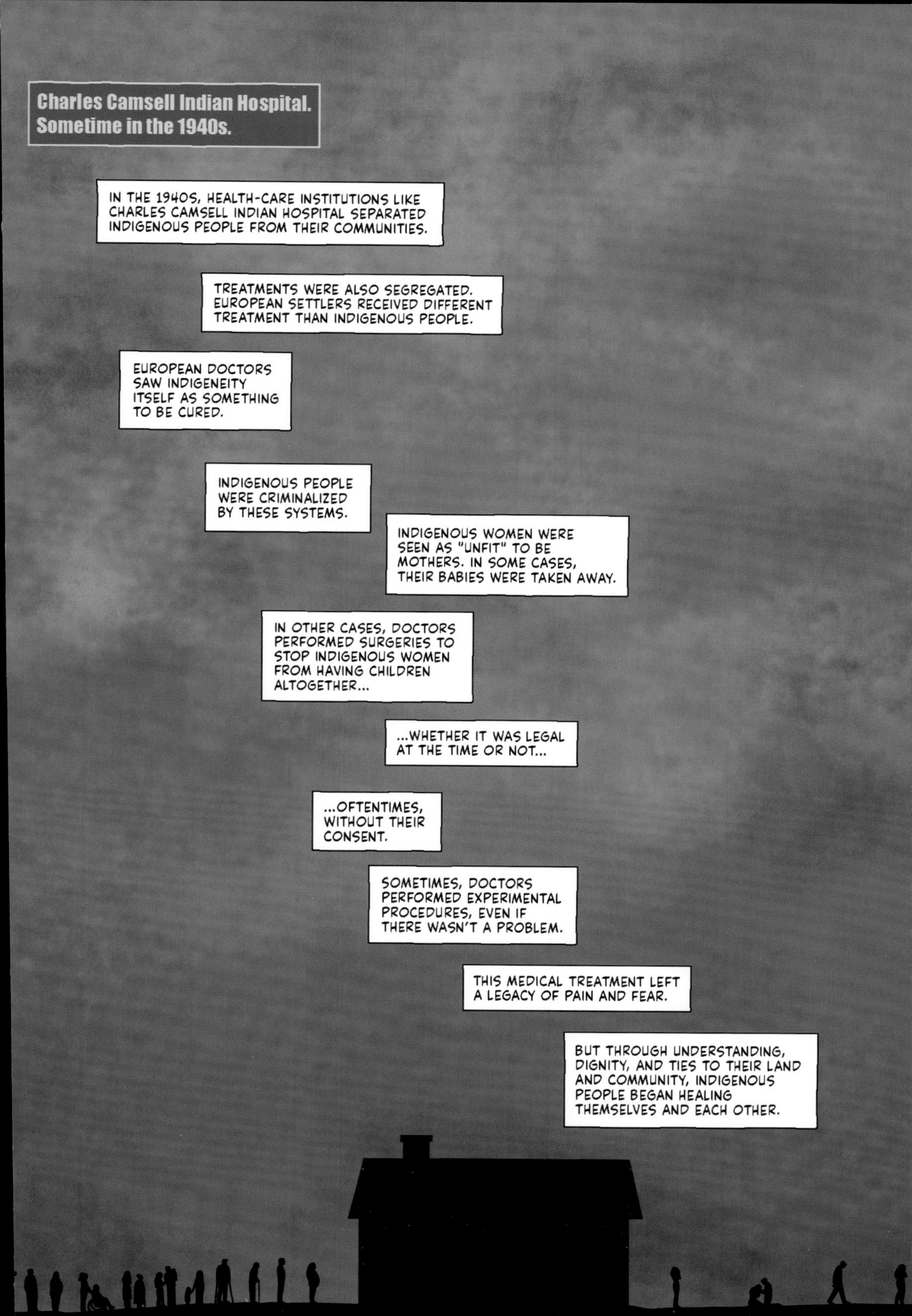
Charles Camsell Indian Hospital. Sometime in the 1940s.
IN THE 1940S, HEALTH-CARE INSTITUTIONS LIKE CHARLES CAMSELL INDIAN HOSPITAL SEPARATED INDIGENOUS PEOPLE FROM THEIR COMMUNITIES.
TREATMENTS WERE ALSO SEGREGATED. EUROPEAN SETTLERS RECEIVED DIFFERENT TREATMENT THAN INDIGENOUS PEOPLE.
EUROPEAN DOCTORS SAW INDIGENEITY ITSELF AS SOMETHING TO BE CURED.
INDIGENOUS PEOPLE WERE CRIMINALIZED BY THESE SYSTEMS.
INDIGENOUS WOMEN WERE SEEN AS "UNFIT" TO BE MOTHERS. IN SOME CASES, THEIR BABIES WERE TAKEN AWAY.
IN OTHER CASES, DOCTORS PERFORMED SURGERIES TO STOP INDIGENOUS WOMEN FROM HAVING CHILDREN ALTOGETHER...
...WHETHER IT WAS LEGAL AT THE TIME OR NOT...
...OFTENTIMES, WITHOUT THEIR CONSENT.
SOMETIMES, DOCTORS PERFORMED EXPERIMENTAL PROCEDURES, EVEN IF THERE WASN'T A PROBLEM.
THIS MEDICAL TREATMENT LEFT A LEGACY OF PAIN AND FEAR.
BUT THROUGH UNDERSTANDING, DIGNITY, AND TIES TO THEIR LAND AND COMMUNITY, INDIGENOUS PEOPLE BEGAN HEALING THEMSELVES AND EACH OTHER.

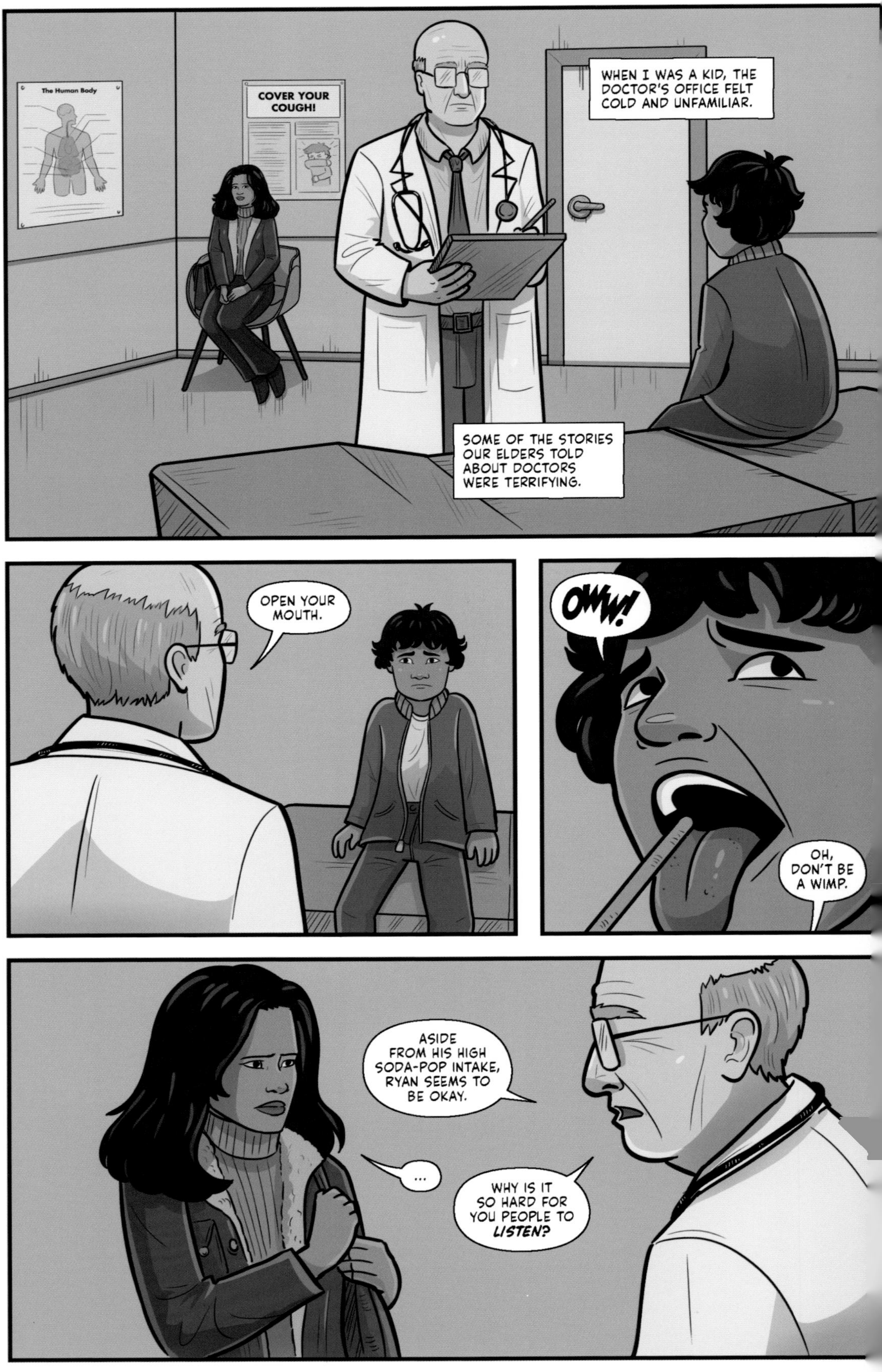
The Human Body
COVER YOUR COUGH!
WHEN I WAS A KID, THE DOCTOR'S OFFICE FELT COLD AND UNFAMILIAR.
SOME OF THE STORIES OUR ELDERS TOLD ABOUT DOCTORS WERE TERRIFYING.
OPEN YOUR MOUTH.
OWW!
OH, DON'T BE A WIMP.
ASIDE FROM HIS HIGH SODA-POP INTAKE, RYAN SEEMS TO BE OKAY.
...
WHY IS IT SO HARD FOR YOU PEOPLE TO *LISTEN?*

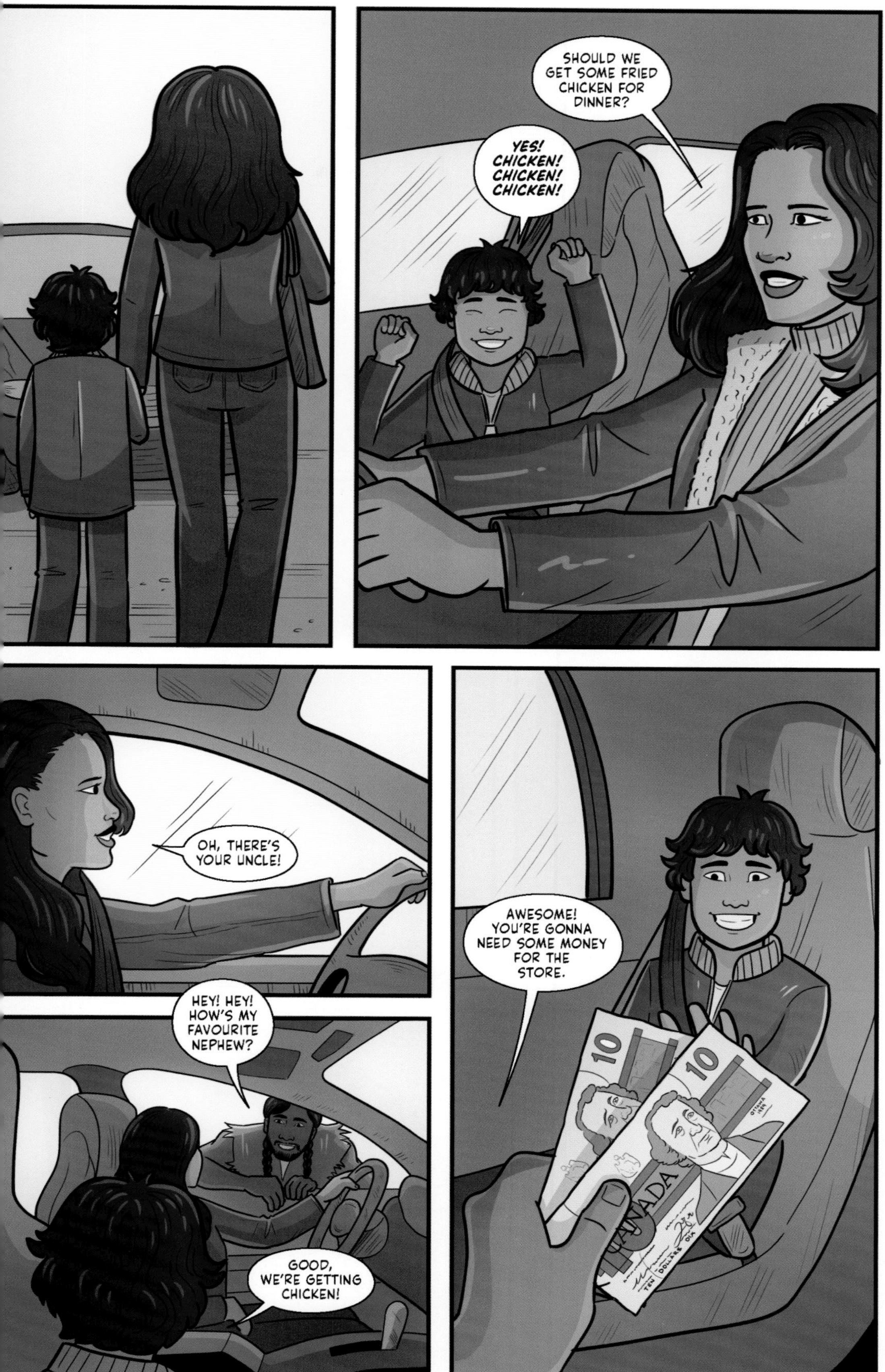
SHOULD WE GET SOME FRIED CHICKEN FOR DINNER?
YES! CHICKEN! CHICKEN! CHICKEN!
OH, THERE'S YOUR UNCLE!
HEY! HEY! HOW'S MY FAVOURITE NEPHEW?
GOOD, WE'RE GETTING CHICKEN!
AWESOME! YOU'RE GONNA NEED SOME MONEY FOR THE STORE.
10
10
CANADA

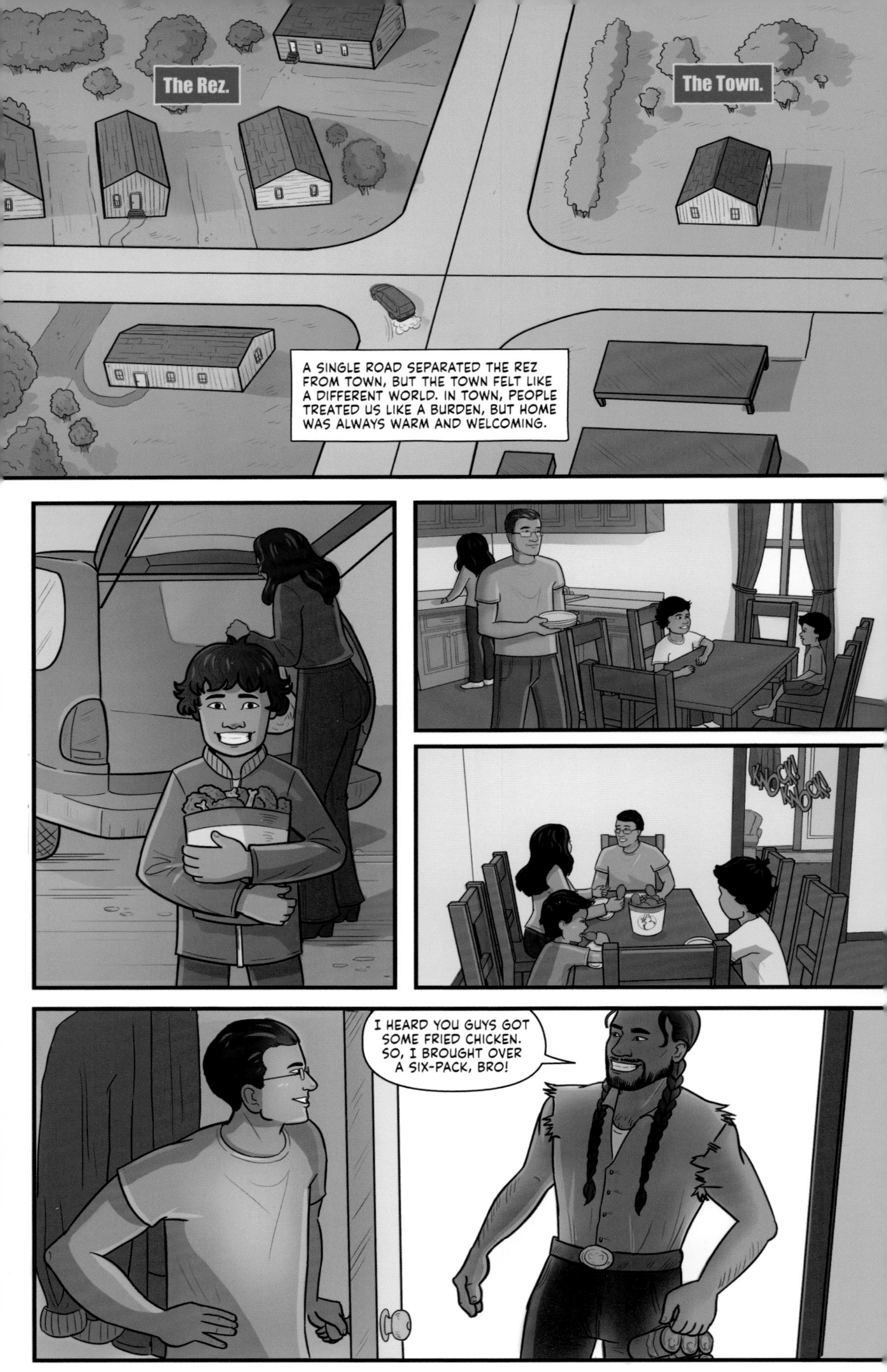
The Rez.
The Town.
A SINGLE ROAD SEPARATED THE REZ FROM TOWN, BUT THE TOWN FELT LIKE A DIFFERENT WORLD. IN TOWN, PEOPLE TREATED US LIKE A BURDEN, BUT HOME WAS ALWAYS WARM AND WELCOMING.
KNOCK! KNOCK!
I HEARD YOU GUYS GOT SOME FRIED CHICKEN. SO, I BROUGHT OVER A SIX-PACK, BRO!

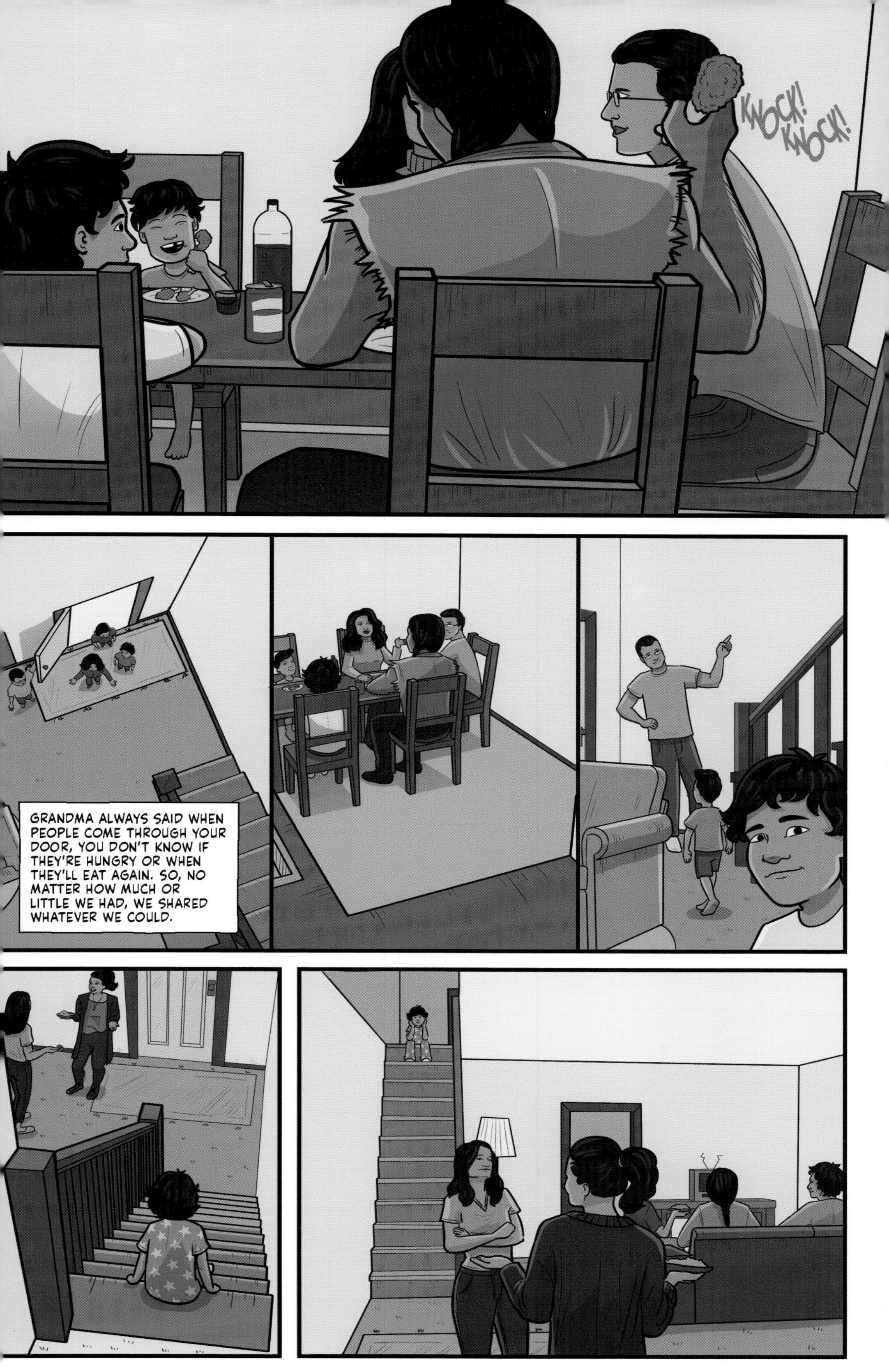
KNOCK! KNOCK!
GRANDMA ALWAYS SAID WHEN PEOPLE COME THROUGH YOUR DOOR, YOU DON'T KNOW IF THEY'RE HUNGRY OR WHEN THEY'LL EAT AGAIN. SO, NO MATTER HOW MUCH OR LITTLE WE HAD, WE SHARED WHATEVER WE COULD.

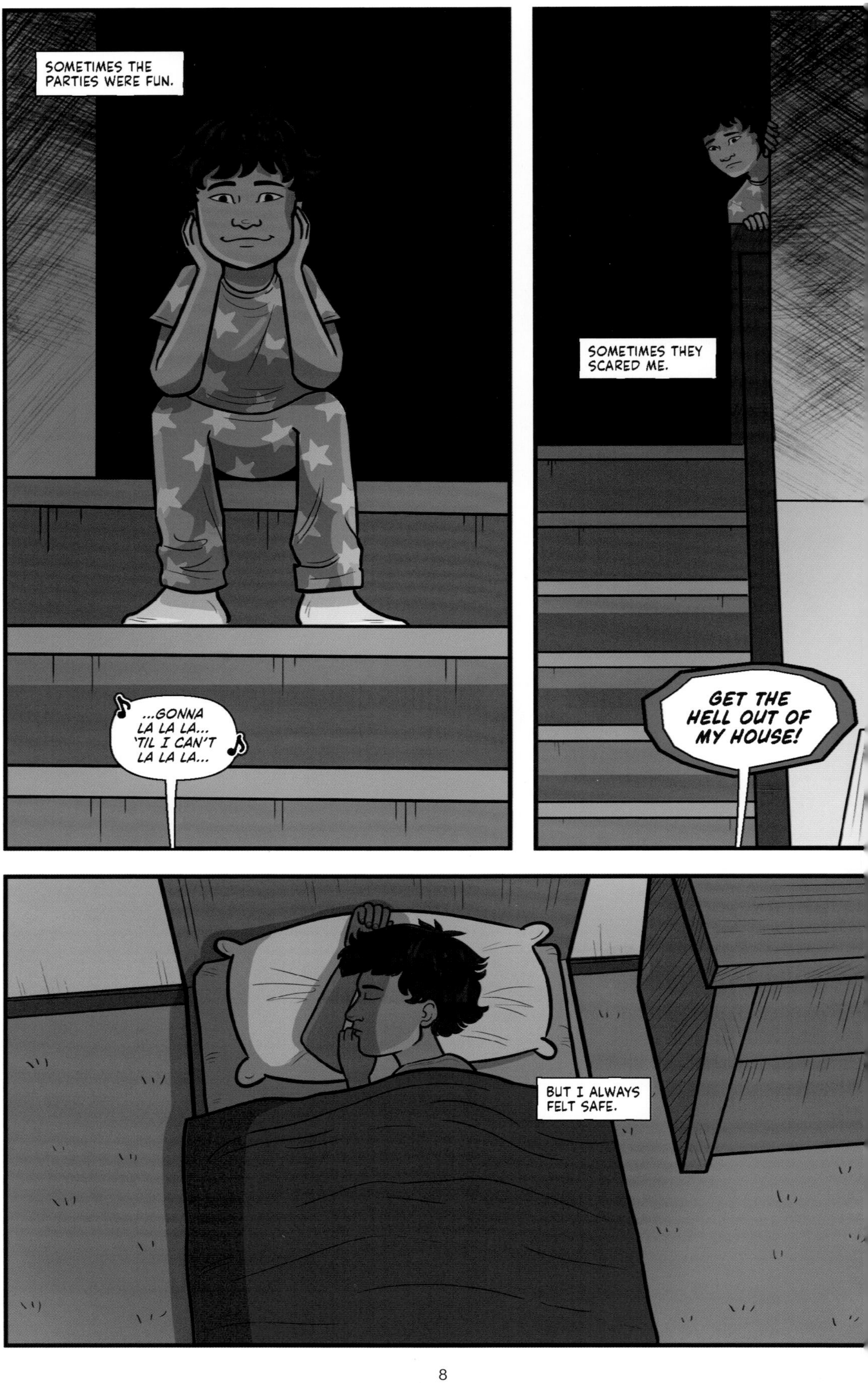
SOMETIMES THE PARTIES WERE FUN.
...GONNA LA LA LA... 'TIL I CAN'T LA LA LA...
SOMETIMES THEY SCARED ME.
GET THE HELL OUT OF MY HOUSE!
BUT I ALWAYS FELT SAFE.

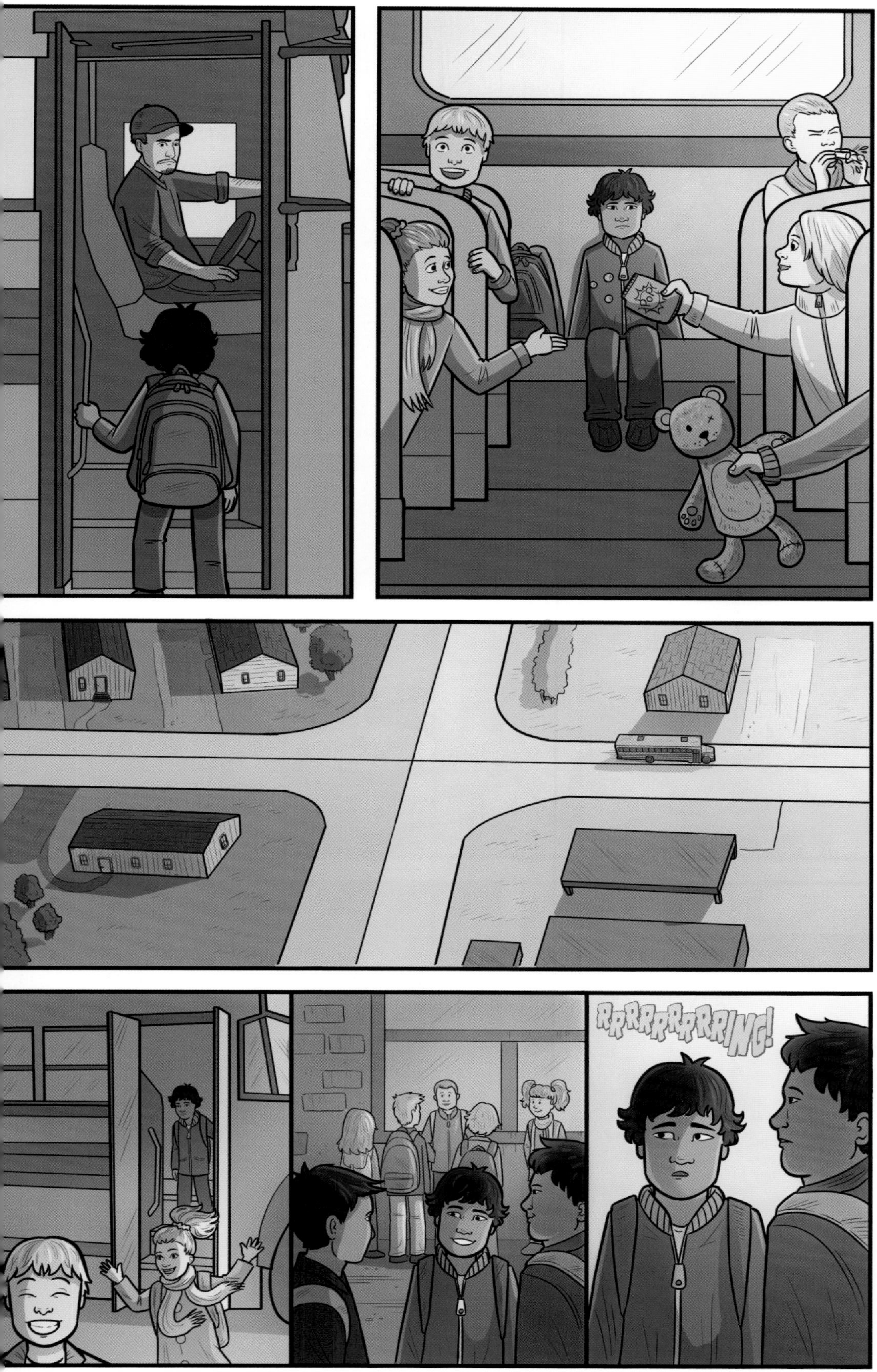
RRRRRRRRRING!

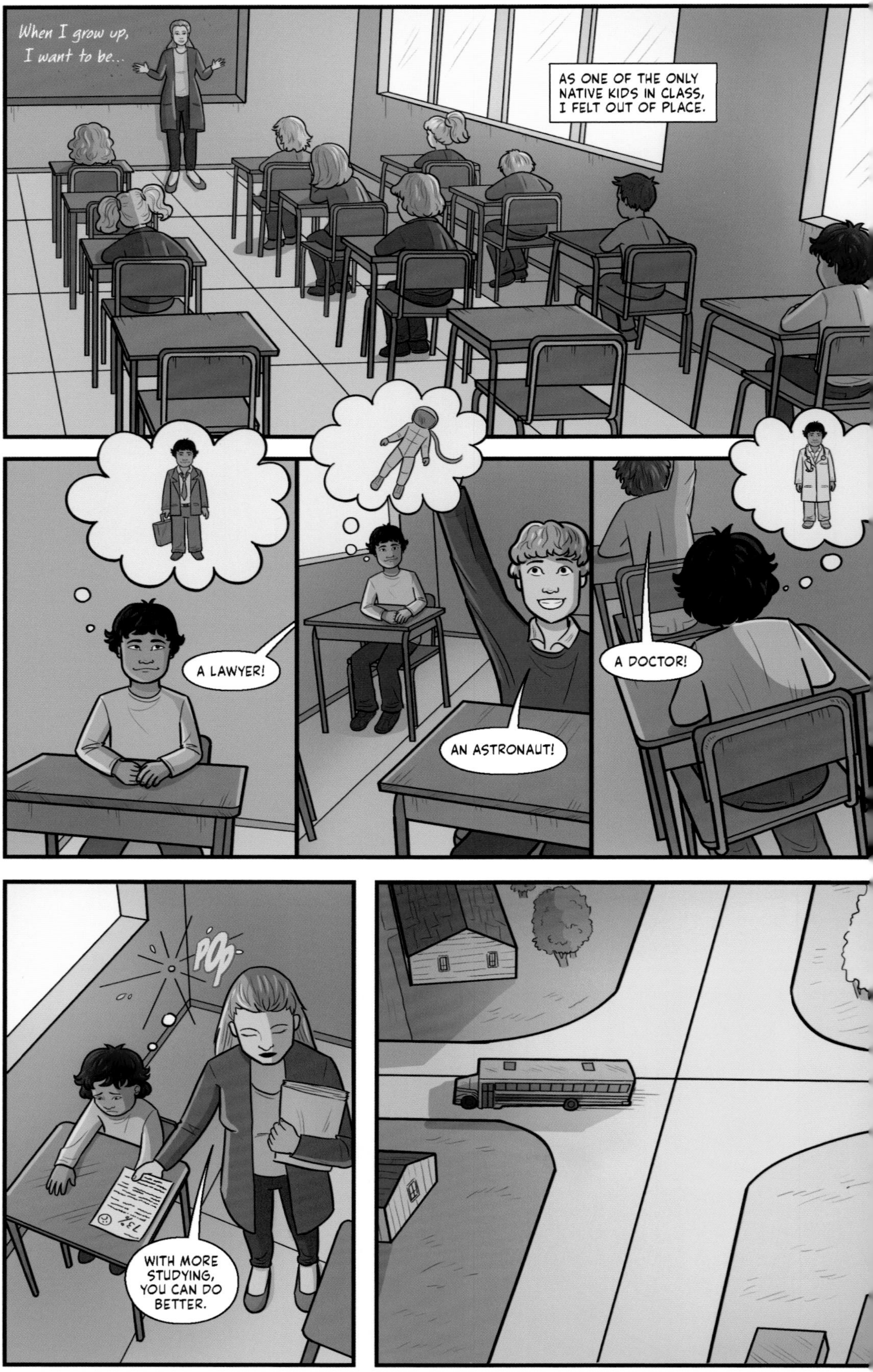

When I grow up, I want to be...
AS ONE OF THE ONLY NATIVE KIDS IN CLASS, I FELT OUT OF PLACE.
A LAWYER!
AN ASTRONAUT!
A DOCTOR!
POP
WITH MORE STUDYING, YOU CAN DO BETTER.

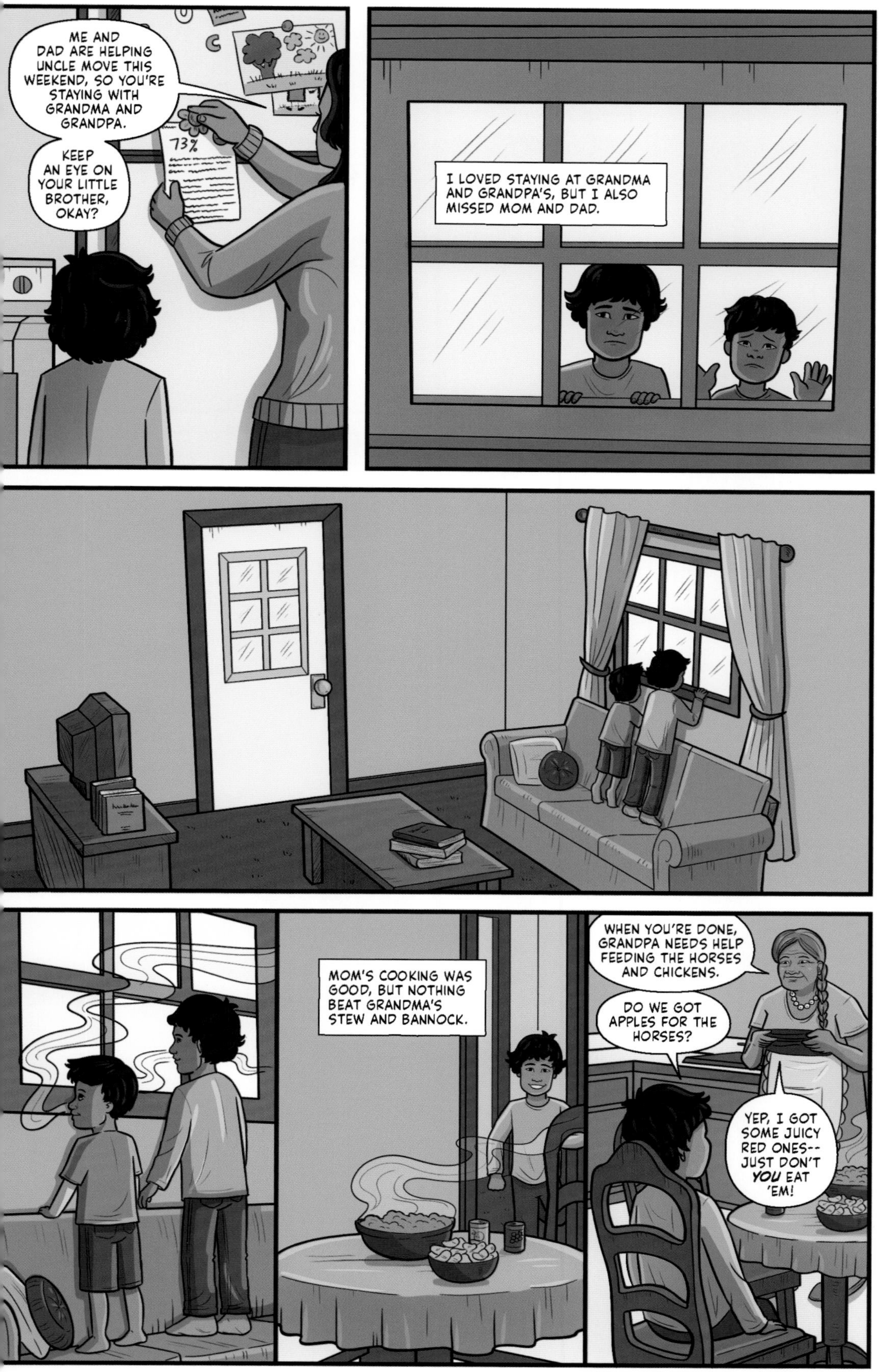
ME AND DAD ARE HELPING UNCLE MOVE THIS WEEKEND, SO YOU'RE STAYING WITH GRANDMA AND GRANDPA.
KEEP AN EYE ON YOUR LITTLE BROTHER, OKAY?
73%
I LOVED STAYING AT GRANDMA AND GRANDPA'S, BUT I ALSO MISSED MOM AND DAD.
MOM'S COOKING WAS GOOD, BUT NOTHING BEAT GRANDMA'S STEW AND BANNOCK.
WHEN YOU'RE DONE, GRANDPA NEEDS HELP FEEDING THE HORSES AND CHICKENS.
DO WE GOT APPLES FOR THE HORSES?
YEP, I GOT SOME JUICY RED ONES-- JUST DON'T *YOU* EAT 'EM!

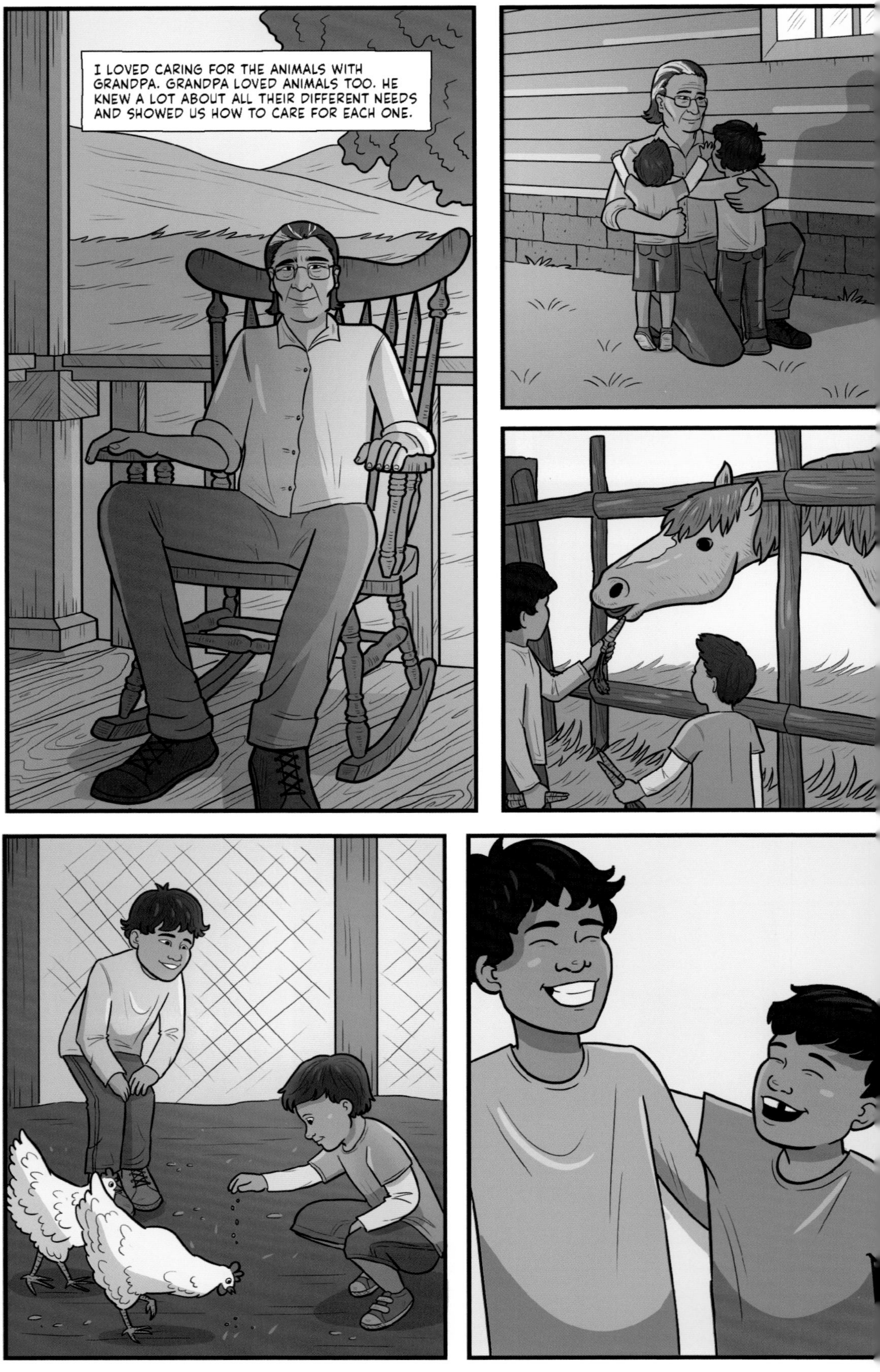
I LOVED CARING FOR THE ANIMALS WITH GRANDPA. GRANDPA LOVED ANIMALS TOO. HE KNEW A LOT ABOUT ALL THEIR DIFFERENT NEEDS AND SHOWED US HOW TO CARE FOR EACH ONE.

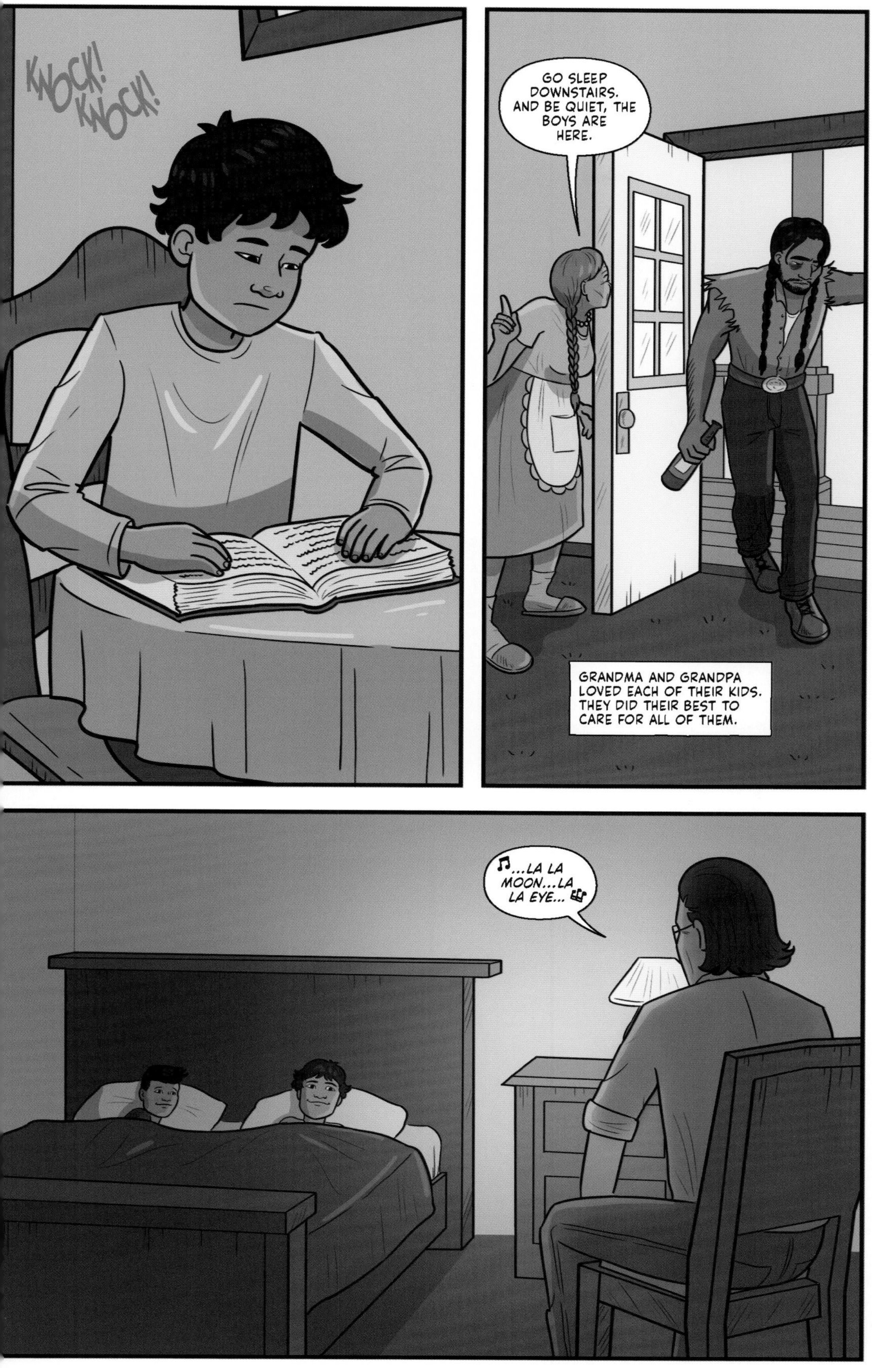
KNOCK! KNOCK!
GO SLEEP DOWNSTAIRS. AND BE QUIET, THE BOYS ARE HERE.
GRANDMA AND GRANDPA LOVED EACH OF THEIR KIDS. THEY DID THEIR BEST TO CARE FOR ALL OF THEM.
♫...LA LA MOON...LA LA EYE... ♫

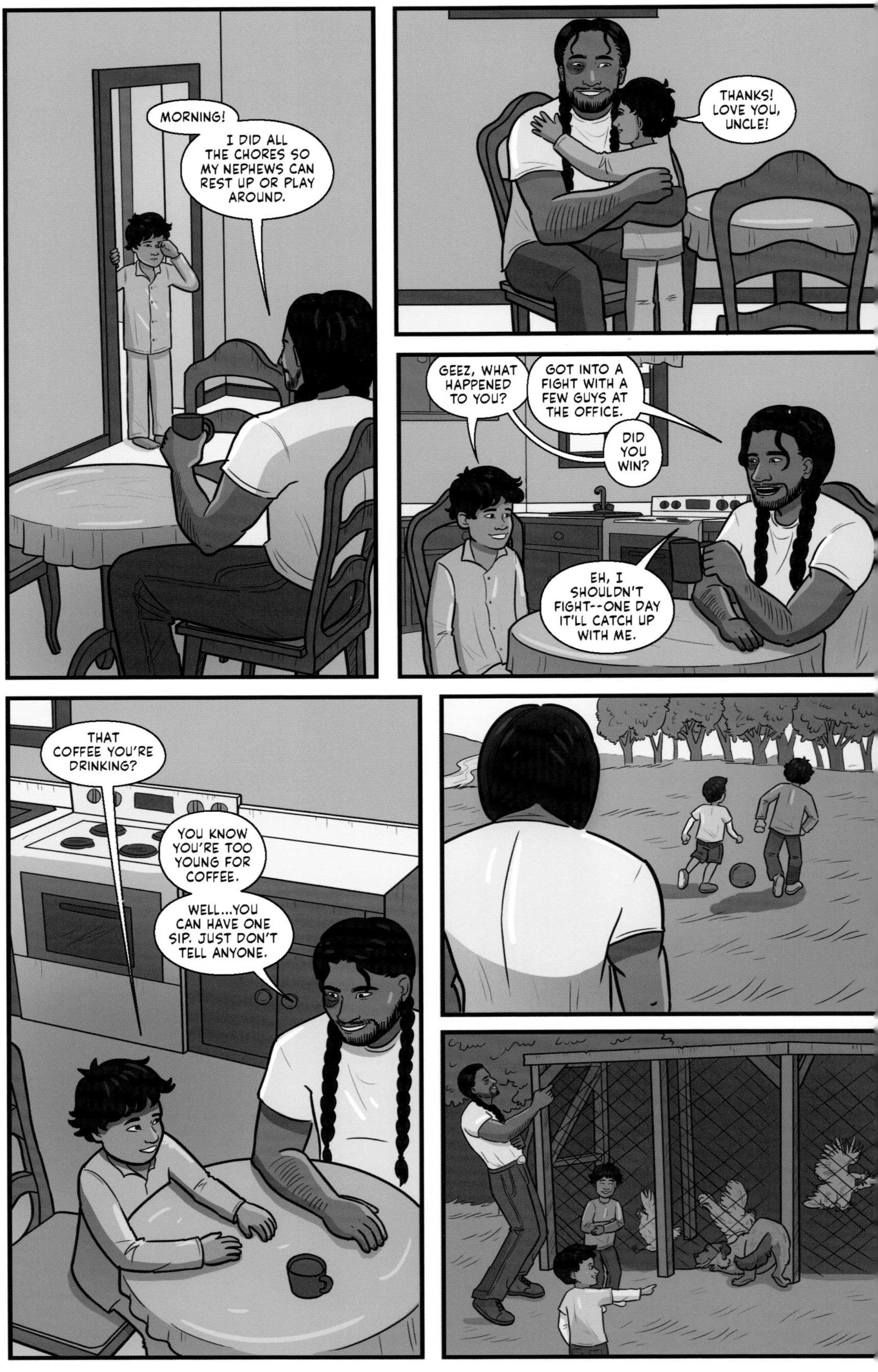
MORNING!
I DID ALL THE CHORES SO MY NEPHEWS CAN REST UP OR PLAY AROUND.
THANKS! LOVE YOU, UNCLE!
GEEZ, WHAT HAPPENED TO YOU?
GOT INTO A FIGHT WITH A FEW GUYS AT THE OFFICE.
DID YOU WIN?
EH, I SHOULDN'T FIGHT--ONE DAY IT'LL CATCH UP WITH ME.
THAT COFFEE YOU'RE DRINKING?
YOU KNOW YOU'RE TOO YOUNG FOR COFFEE.
WELL...YOU CAN HAVE ONE SIP. JUST DON'T TELL ANYONE.

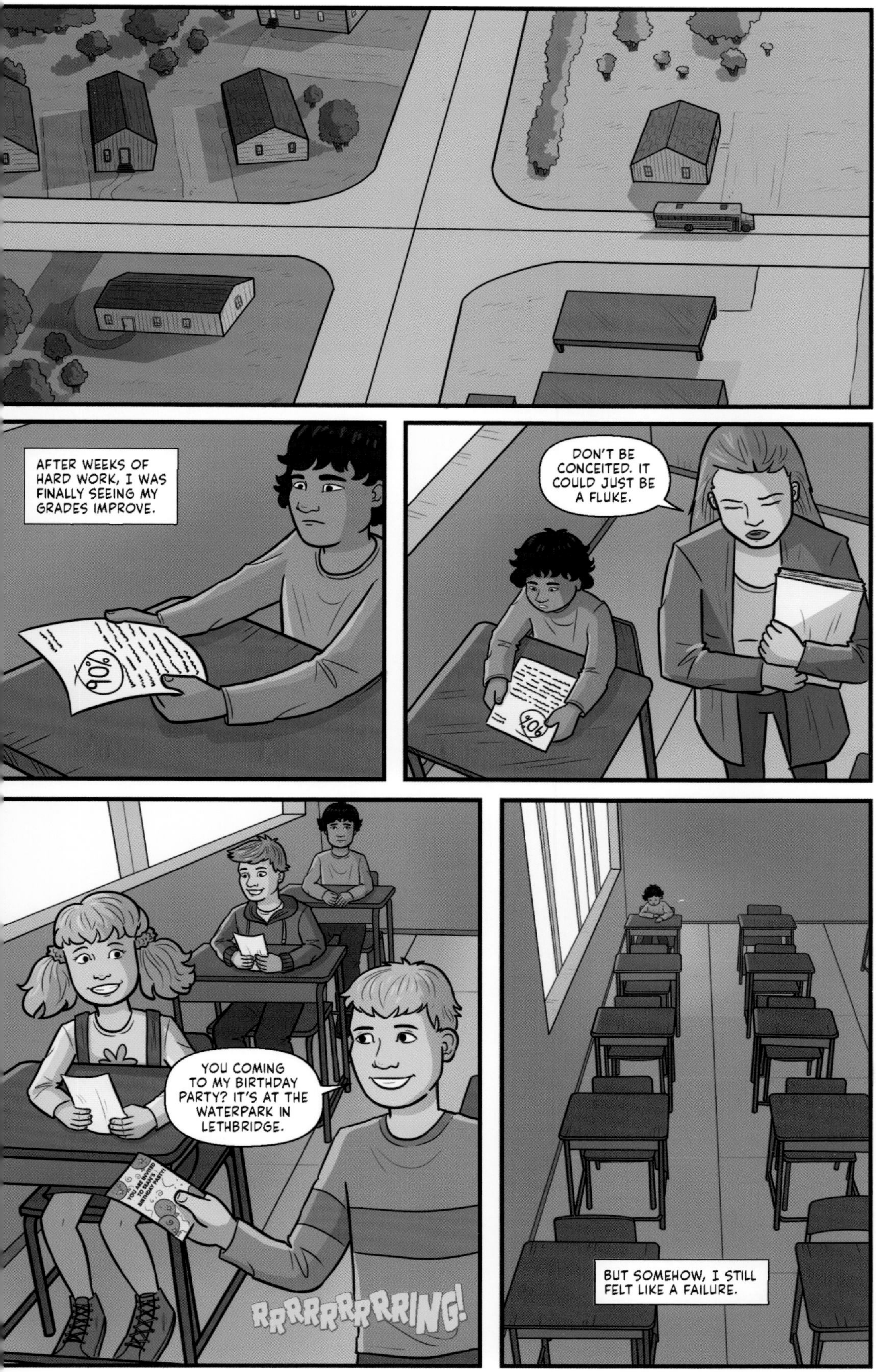
AFTER WEEKS OF HARD WORK, I WAS FINALLY SEEING MY GRADES IMPROVE.
DON'T BE CONCEITED. IT COULD JUST BE A FLUKE.
YOU COMING TO MY BIRTHDAY PARTY? IT'S AT THE WATERPARK IN LETHBRIDGE.
YOU ARE INVITED TO SEAN'S BIRTHDAY PARTY!
RRRRRRRRRING!
BUT SOMEHOW, I STILL FELT LIKE A FAILURE.

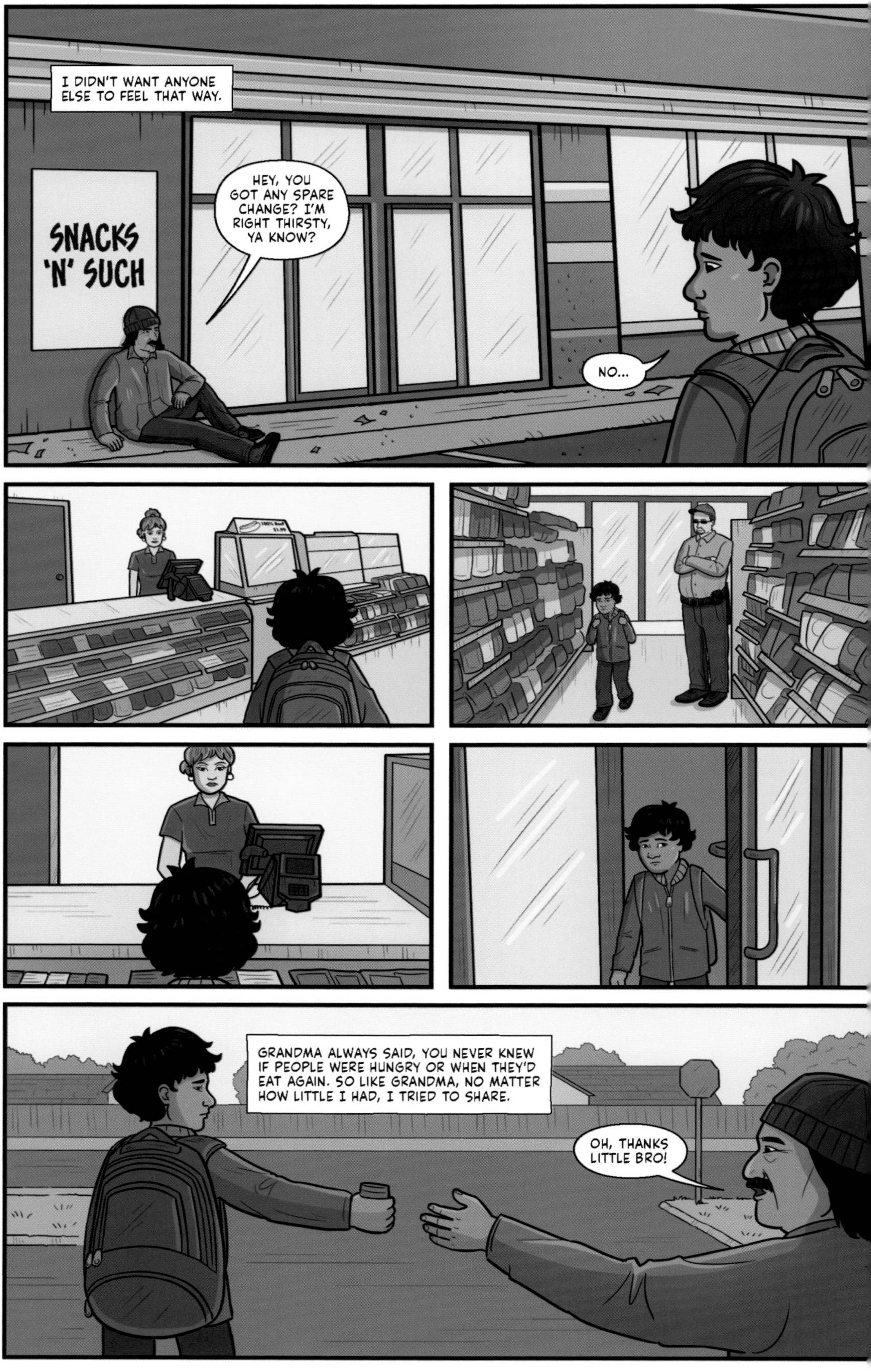
I DIDN'T WANT ANYONE ELSE TO FEEL THAT WAY.
SNACKS 'N' SUCH
HEY, YOU GOT ANY SPARE CHANGE? I'M RIGHT THIRSTY, YA KNOW?
NO...
GRANDMA ALWAYS SAID, YOU NEVER KNEW IF PEOPLE WERE HUNGRY OR WHEN THEY'D EAT AGAIN. SO LIKE GRANDMA, NO MATTER HOW LITTLE I HAD, I TRIED TO SHARE.
OH, THANKS LITTLE BRO!

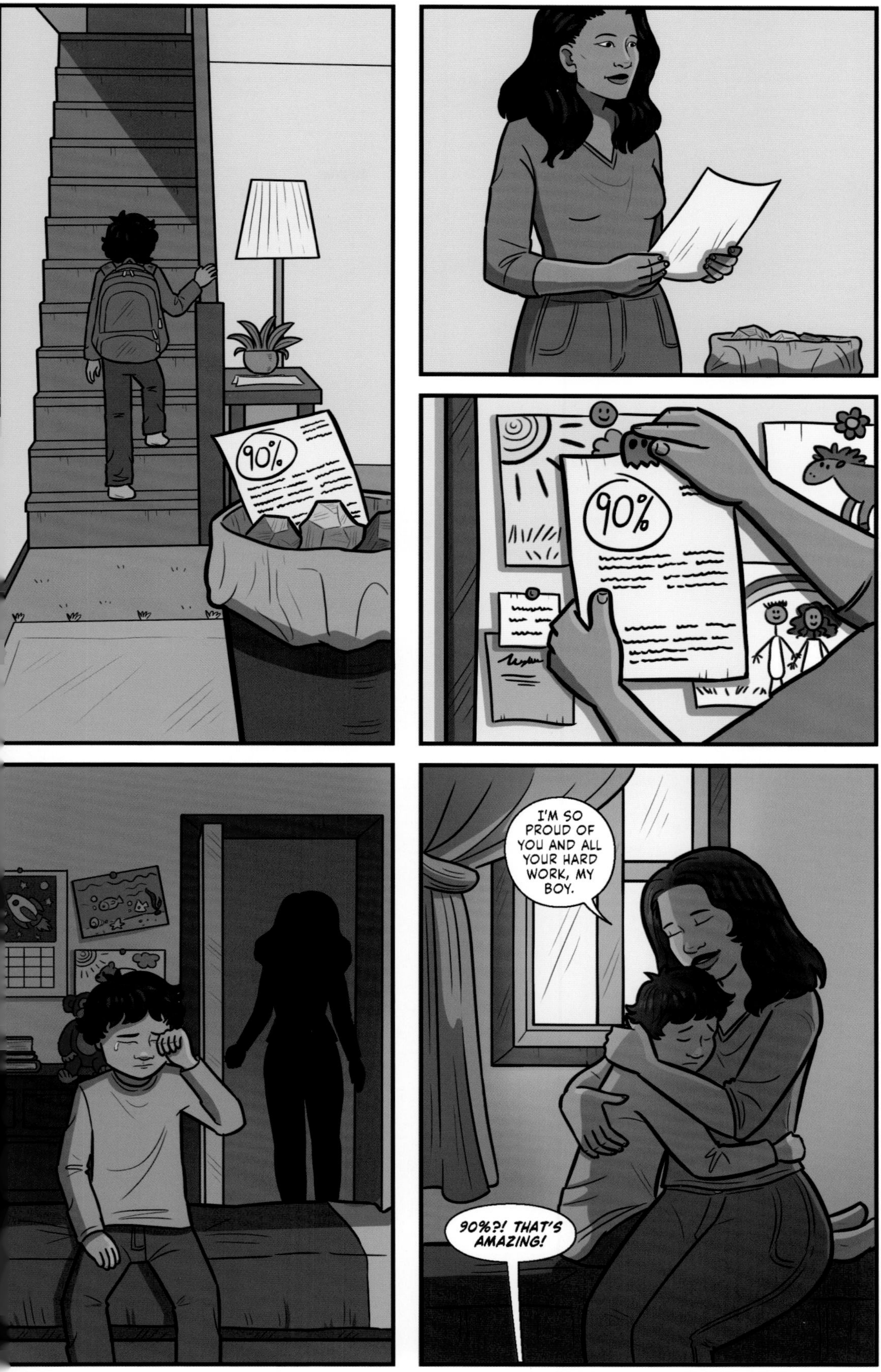
90%
90%
I'M SO PROUD OF YOU AND ALL YOUR HARD WORK, MY BOY.
90%?! THAT'S AMAZING!

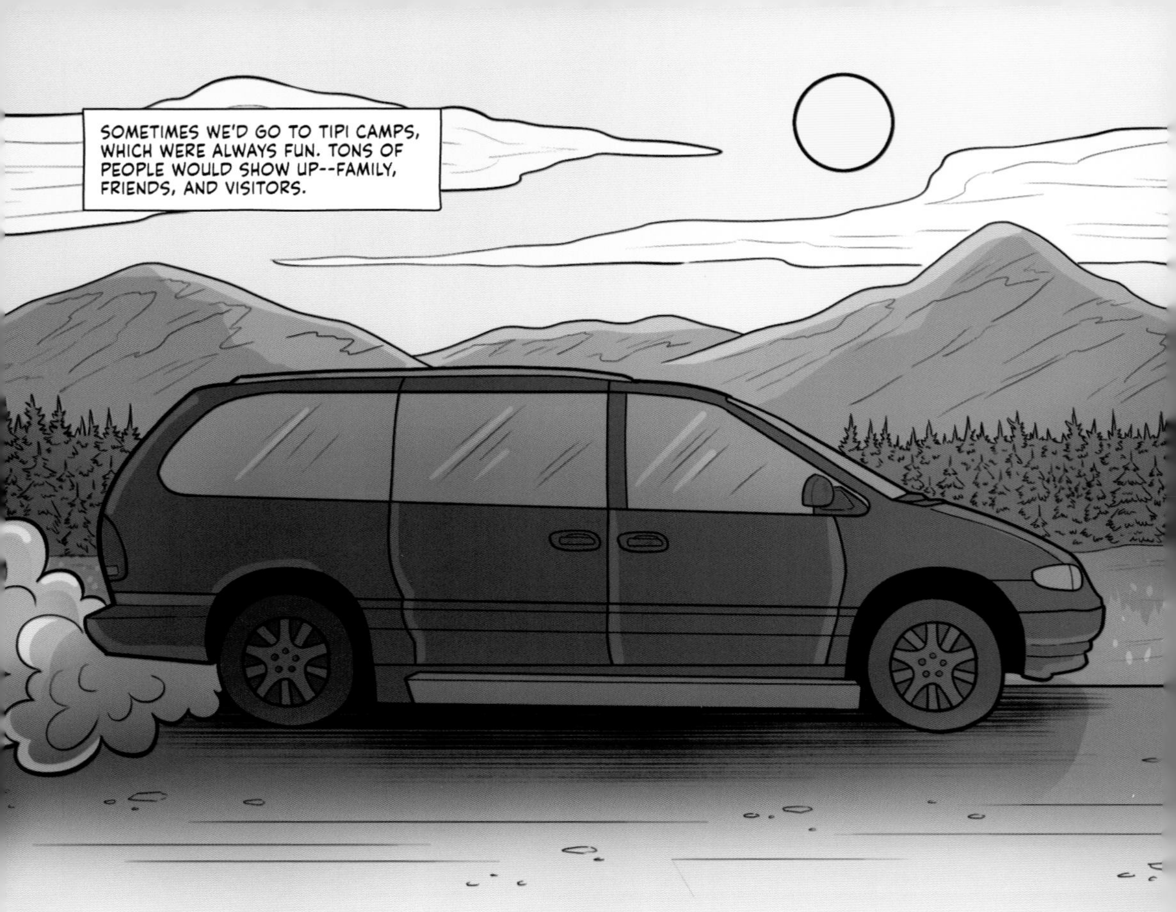
SOMETIMES WE'D GO TO TIPI CAMPS, WHICH WERE ALWAYS FUN. TONS OF PEOPLE WOULD SHOW UP--FAMILY, FRIENDS, AND VISITORS.

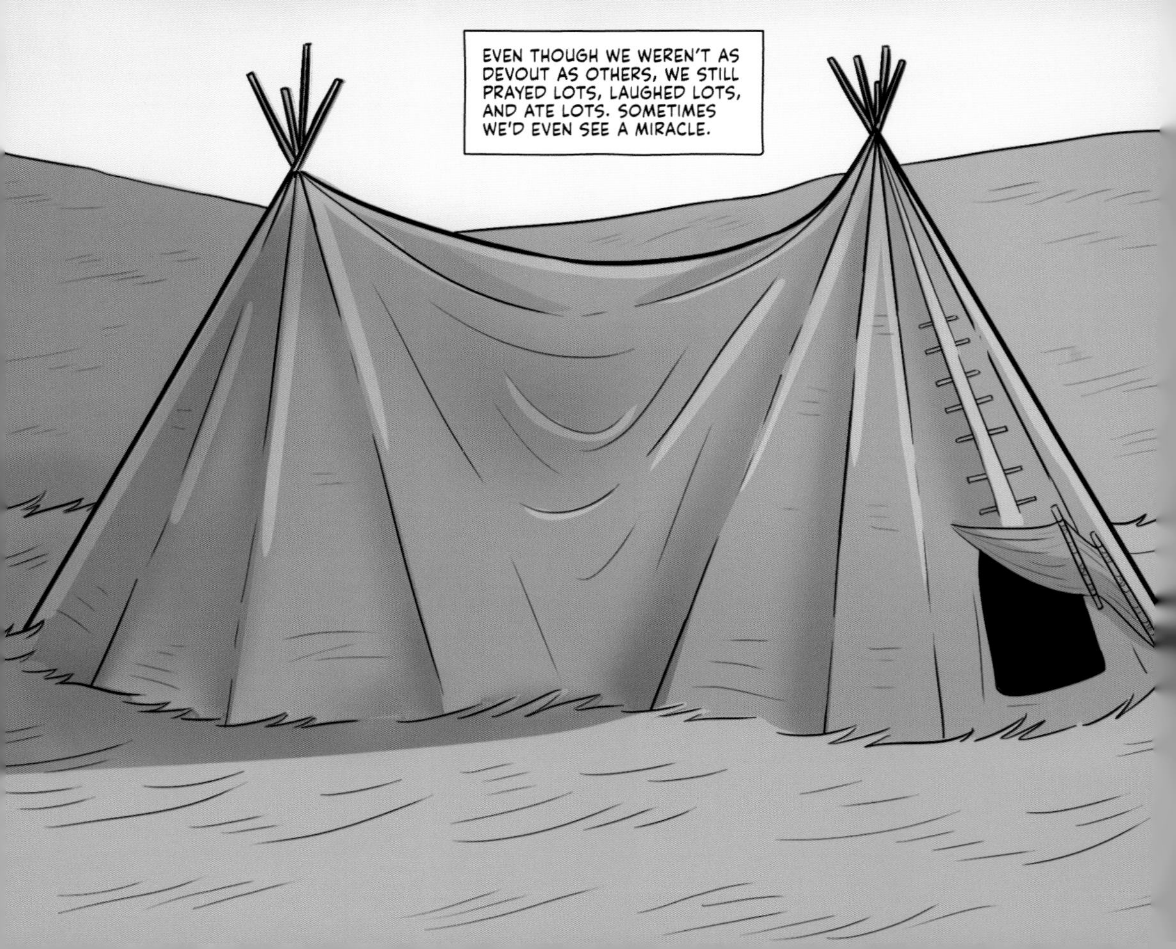
EVEN THOUGH WE WEREN'T AS DEVOUT AS OTHERS, WE STILL PRAYED LOTS, LAUGHED LOTS, AND ATE LOTS. SOMETIMES WE'D EVEN SEE A MIRACLE.

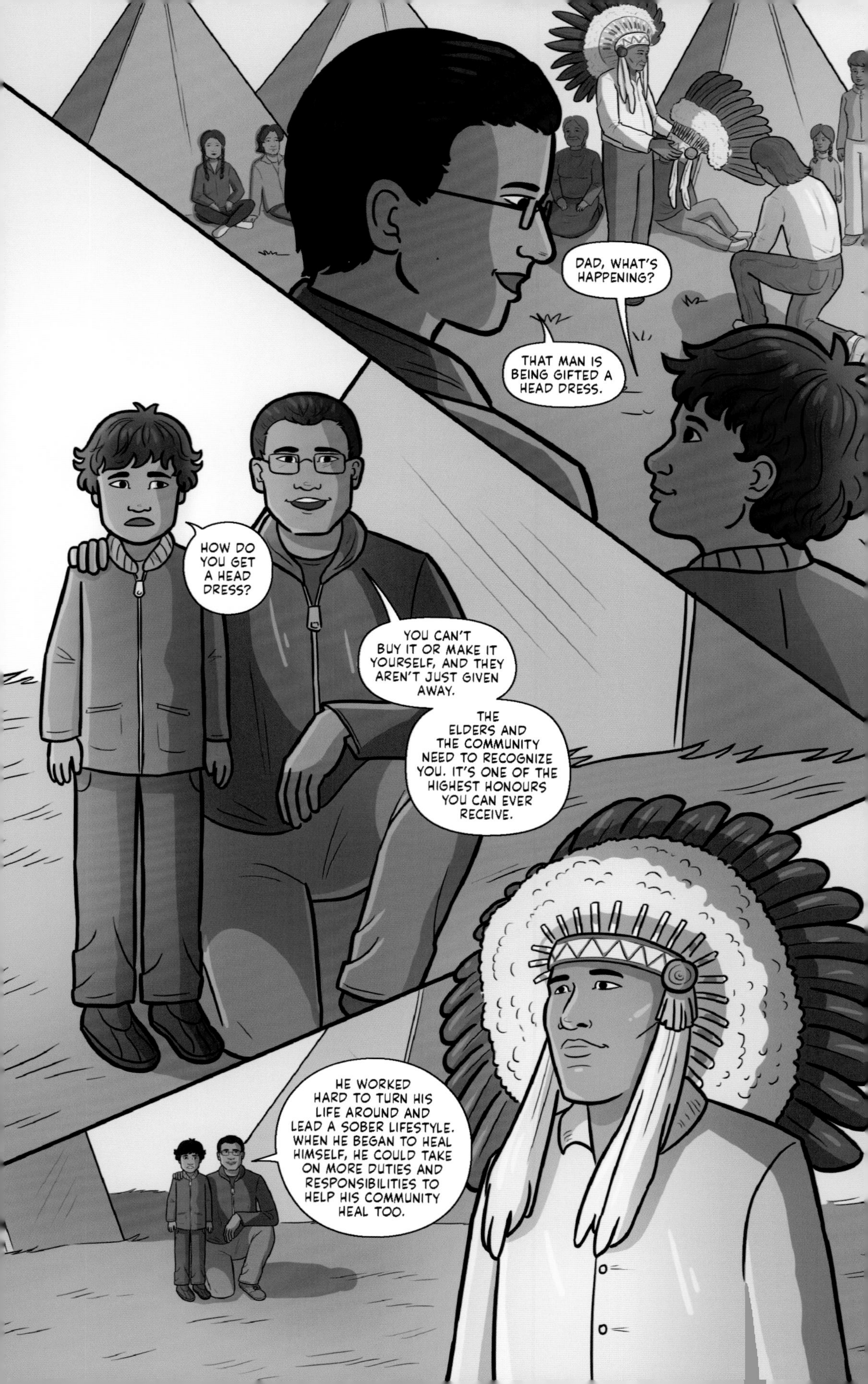
DAD, WHAT'S HAPPENING?
THAT MAN IS BEING GIFTED A HEAD DRESS.
HOW DO YOU GET A HEAD DRESS?
YOU CAN'T BUY IT OR MAKE IT YOURSELF, AND THEY AREN'T JUST GIVEN AWAY.
THE ELDERS AND THE COMMUNITY NEED TO RECOGNIZE YOU. IT'S ONE OF THE HIGHEST HONOURS YOU CAN EVER RECEIVE.
HE WORKED HARD TO TURN HIS LIFE AROUND AND LEAD A SOBER LIFESTYLE. WHEN HE BEGAN TO HEAL HIMSELF, HE COULD TAKE ON MORE DUTIES AND RESPONSIBILITIES TO HELP HIS COMMUNITY HEAL TOO.

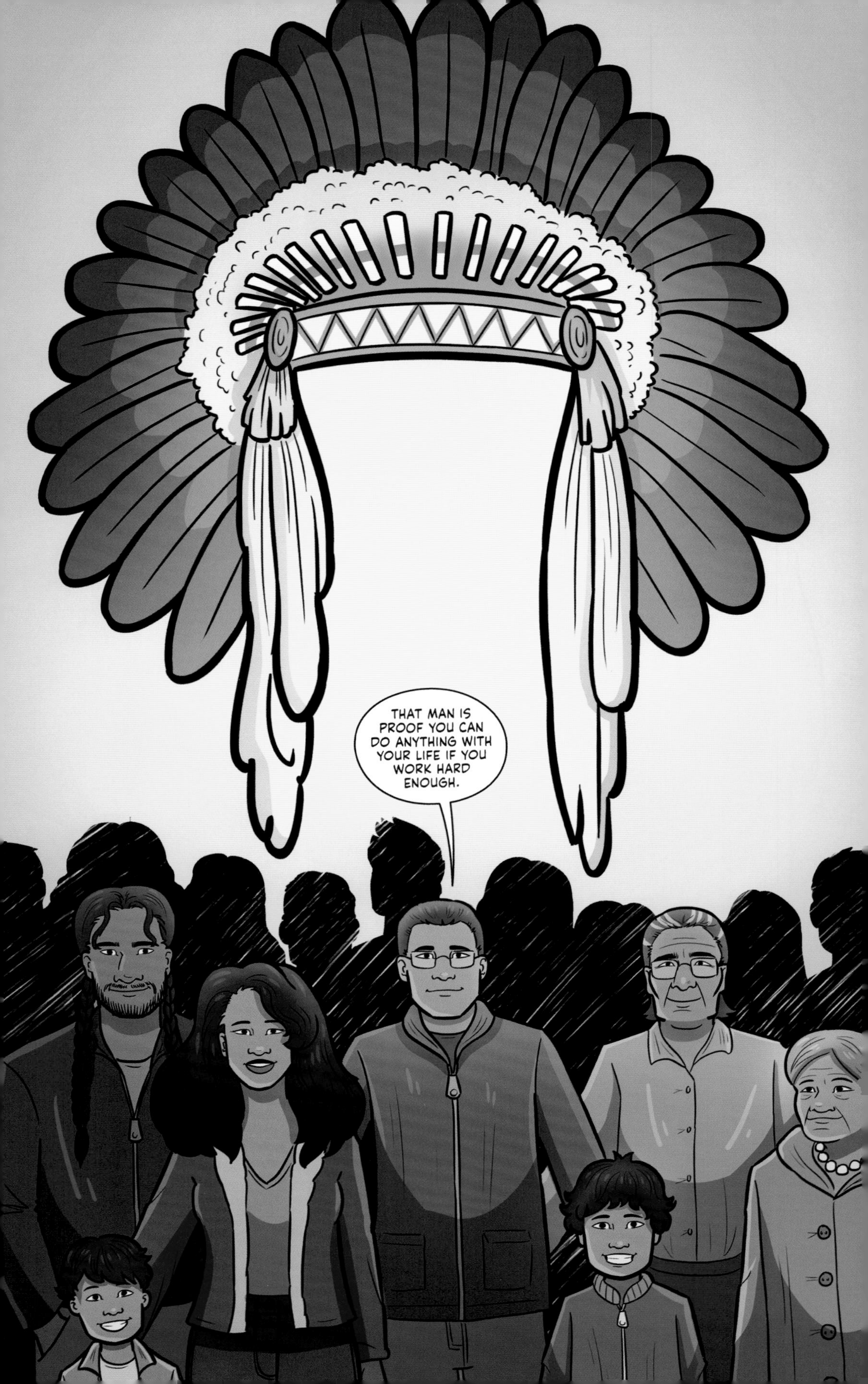
THAT MAN IS PROOF YOU CAN DO ANYTHING WITH YOUR LIFE IF YOU WORK HARD ENOUGH.

Tribal High School.

STUDENTS, PLEASE HELP ME WELCOME A FORMER STUDENT, WHO HAS RECENTLY RETURNED TO OUR COMMUNITY!

OKI NIXOOKOWAX. NI DUN-EH-GO DOCTOR ESTHER TAILFEATHERS.

MY GRANDPA USED TO SAY: "YOU ALWAYS HAVE TO PROVE YOURSELF TO YOUR COMMUNITY."

IT WASN'T AN EASY PATH TO BECOME A DOCTOR--IT WAS HARD WORK! BUT THERE'S NOTHING TO FEAR ABOUT WORKING HARD.

THERE ARE SOME MOMENTS THAT CHANGE YOUR LIFE FOREVER. HEARING DR. ESTHER TAILFEATHERS SPEAK WAS THAT KIND OF MOMENT FOR ME.

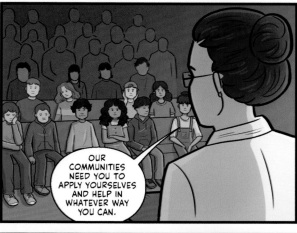

OUR COMMUNITIES NEED YOU TO APPLY YOURSELVES AND HELP IN WHATEVER WAY YOU CAN.

THEY NEED YOU, ALL OF YOU, TO BECOME WARRIORS, PROTECTORS, AND MOST IMPORTANTLY, PROVIDERS FOR THE YOUNG AND THE OLD.

21

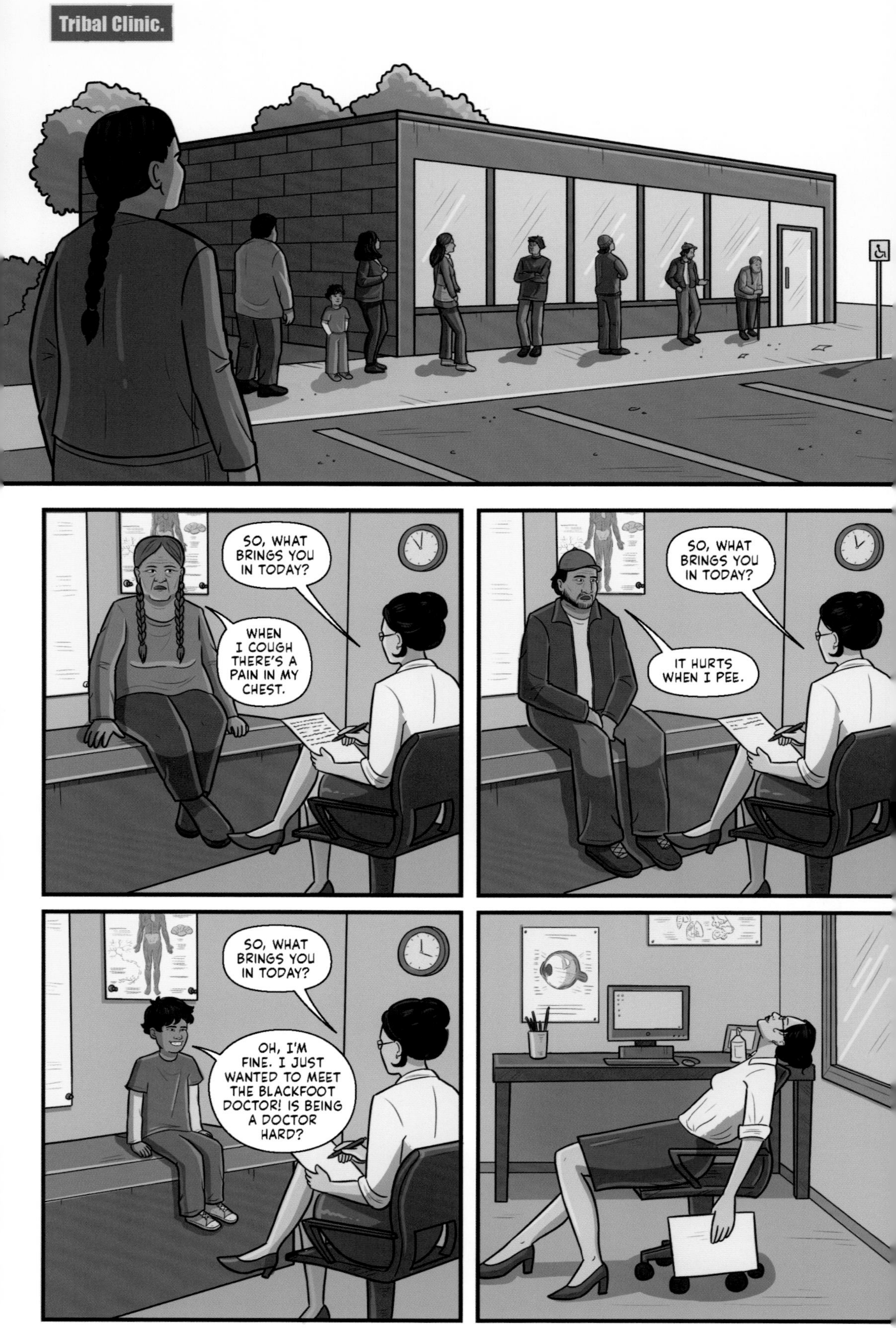
Tribal Clinic.
SO, WHAT BRINGS YOU IN TODAY?
WHEN I COUGH THERE'S A PAIN IN MY CHEST.
SO, WHAT BRINGS YOU IN TODAY?
IT HURTS WHEN I PEE.
SO, WHAT BRINGS YOU IN TODAY?
OH, I'M FINE. I JUST WANTED TO MEET THE BLACKFOOT DOCTOR! IS BEING A DOCTOR HARD?

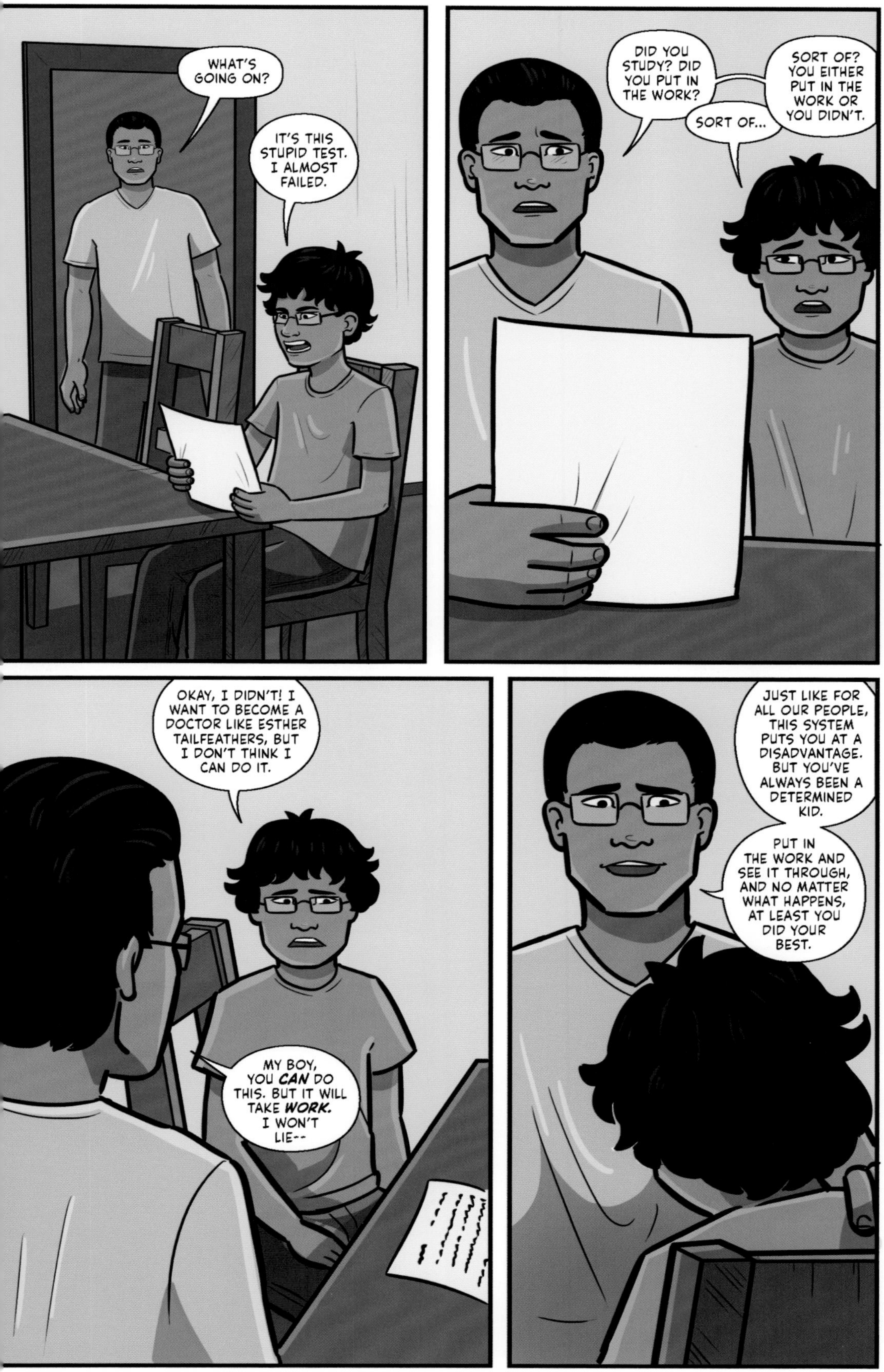
WHAT'S GOING ON?
IT'S THIS STUPID TEST. I ALMOST FAILED.
DID YOU STUDY? DID YOU PUT IN THE WORK?
SORT OF...
SORT OF? YOU EITHER PUT IN THE WORK OR YOU DIDN'T.
OKAY, I DIDN'T! I WANT TO BECOME A DOCTOR LIKE ESTHER TAILFEATHERS, BUT I DON'T THINK I CAN DO IT.
MY BOY, YOU **CAN** DO THIS. BUT IT WILL TAKE **WORK.** I WON'T LIE--
JUST LIKE FOR ALL OUR PEOPLE, THIS SYSTEM PUTS YOU AT A DISADVANTAGE. BUT YOU'VE ALWAYS BEEN A DETERMINED KID.
PUT IN THE WORK AND SEE IT THROUGH, AND NO MATTER WHAT HAPPENS, AT LEAST YOU DID YOUR BEST.

EVEN THOUGH I WAS WORKING HARD, BECOMING A DOCTOR STILL SEEMED LIKE A DISTANT DREAM.

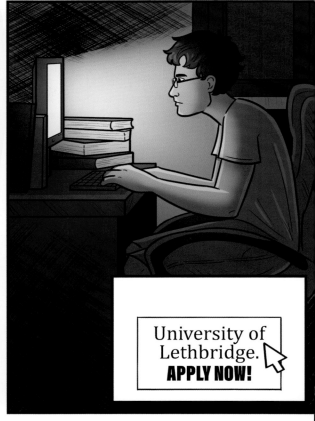

University of Lethbridge.
APPLY NOW!

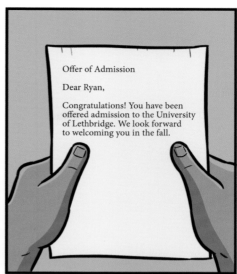

Offer of Admission

Dear Ryan,

Congratulations! You have been offered admission to the University of Lethbridge. We look forward to welcoming you in the fall.

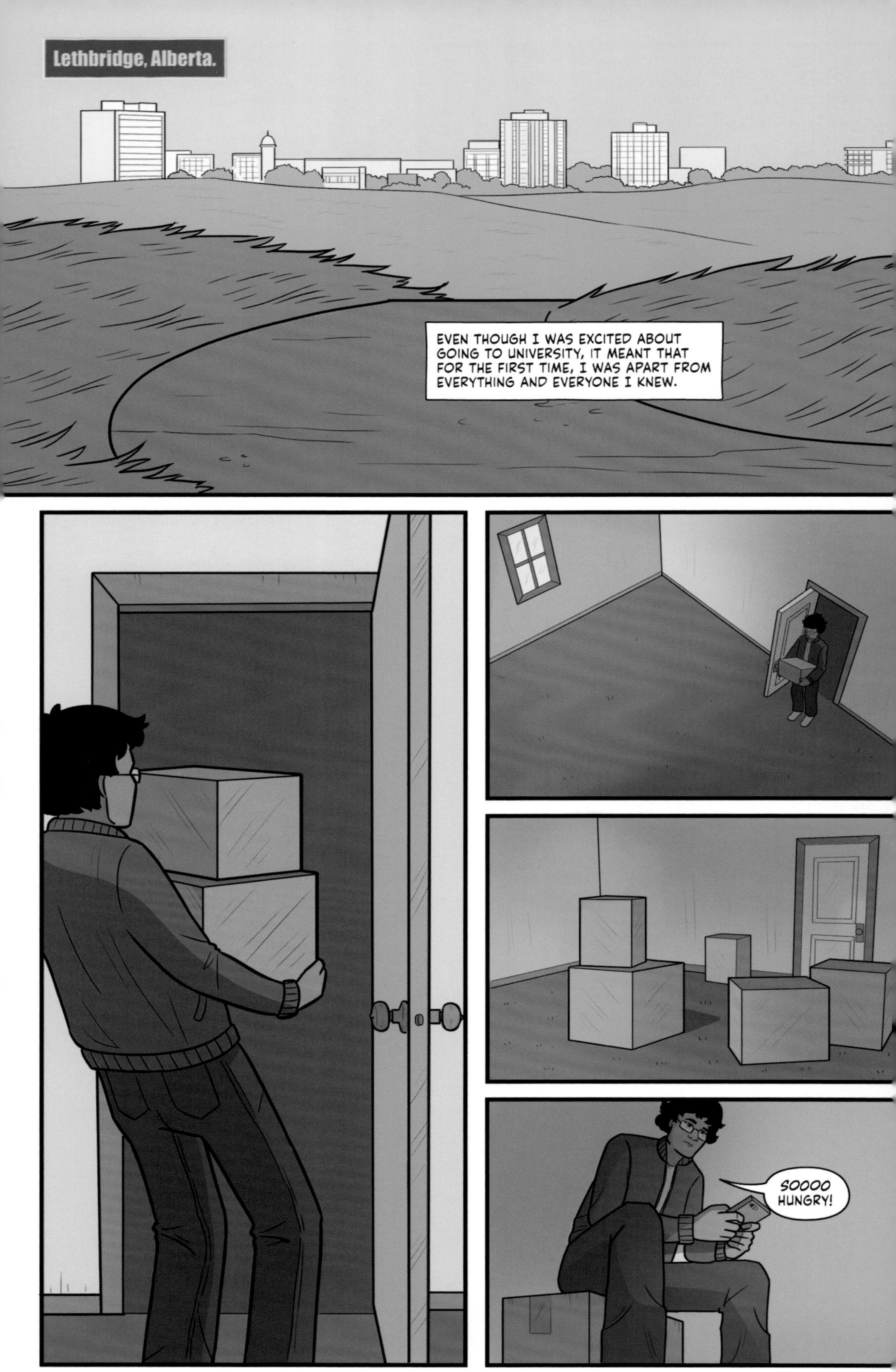
Lethbridge, Alberta.
EVEN THOUGH I WAS EXCITED ABOUT GOING TO UNIVERSITY, IT MEANT THAT FOR THE FIRST TIME, I WAS APART FROM EVERYTHING AND EVERYONE I KNEW.
SOOOO HUNGRY!

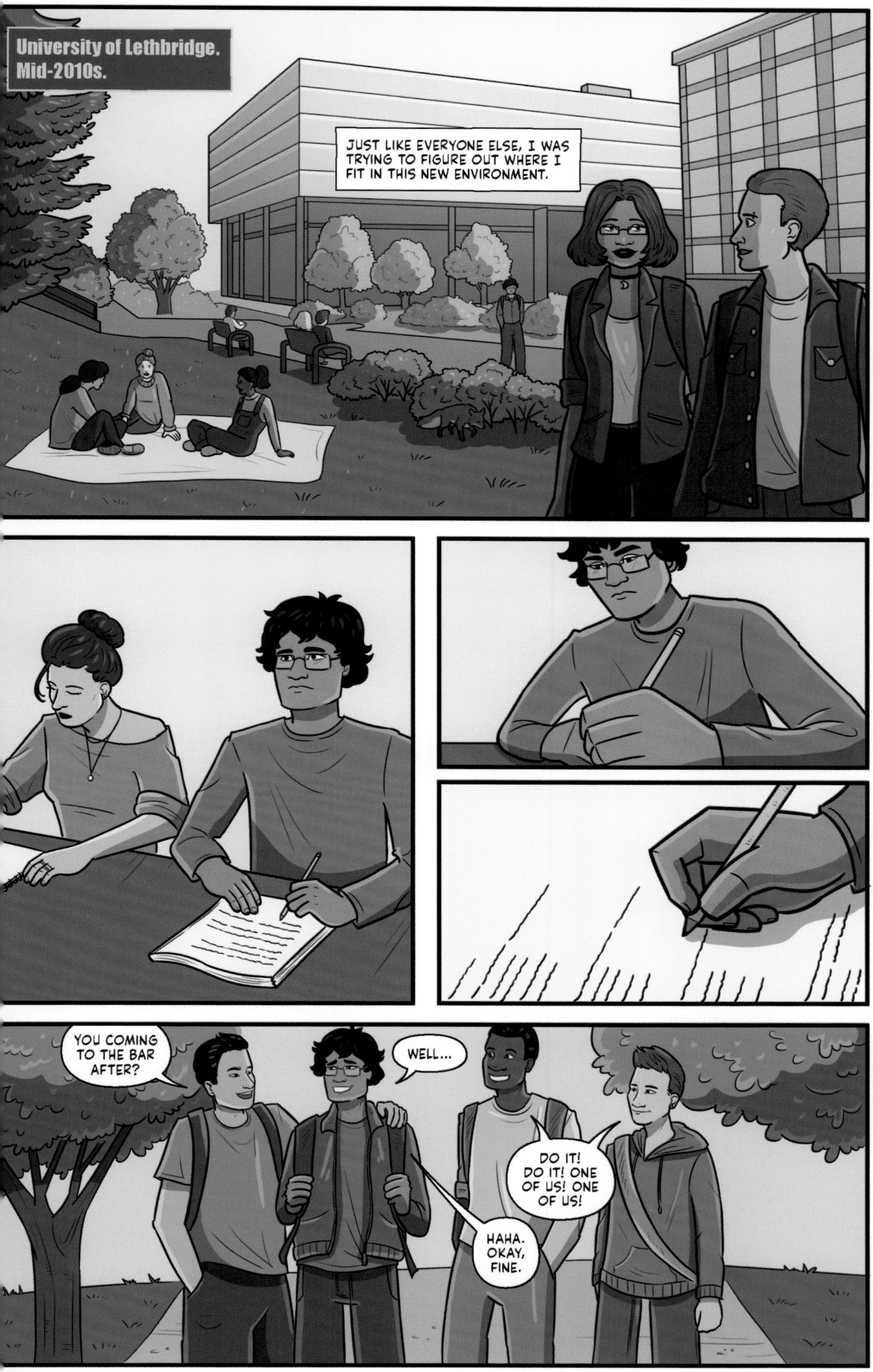
University of Lethbridge. Mid-2010s.
JUST LIKE EVERYONE ELSE, I WAS TRYING TO FIGURE OUT WHERE I FIT IN THIS NEW ENVIRONMENT.
YOU COMING TO THE BAR AFTER?
WELL...
DO IT! DO IT! ONE OF US! ONE OF US!
HAHA. OKAY, FINE.

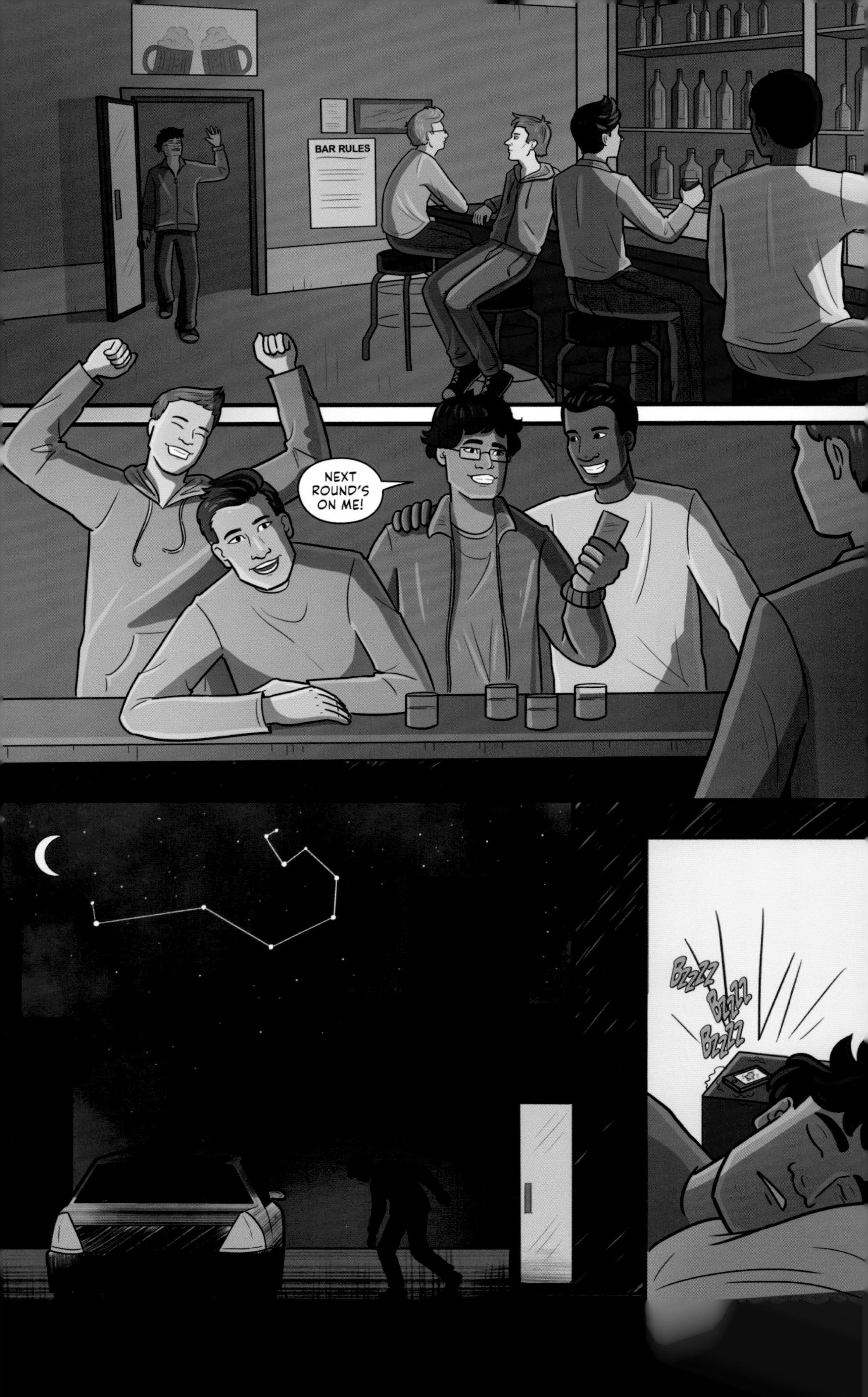
BAR RULES
NEXT ROUND'S ON ME!
Bzzzz
Bzzzz
Bzzzz

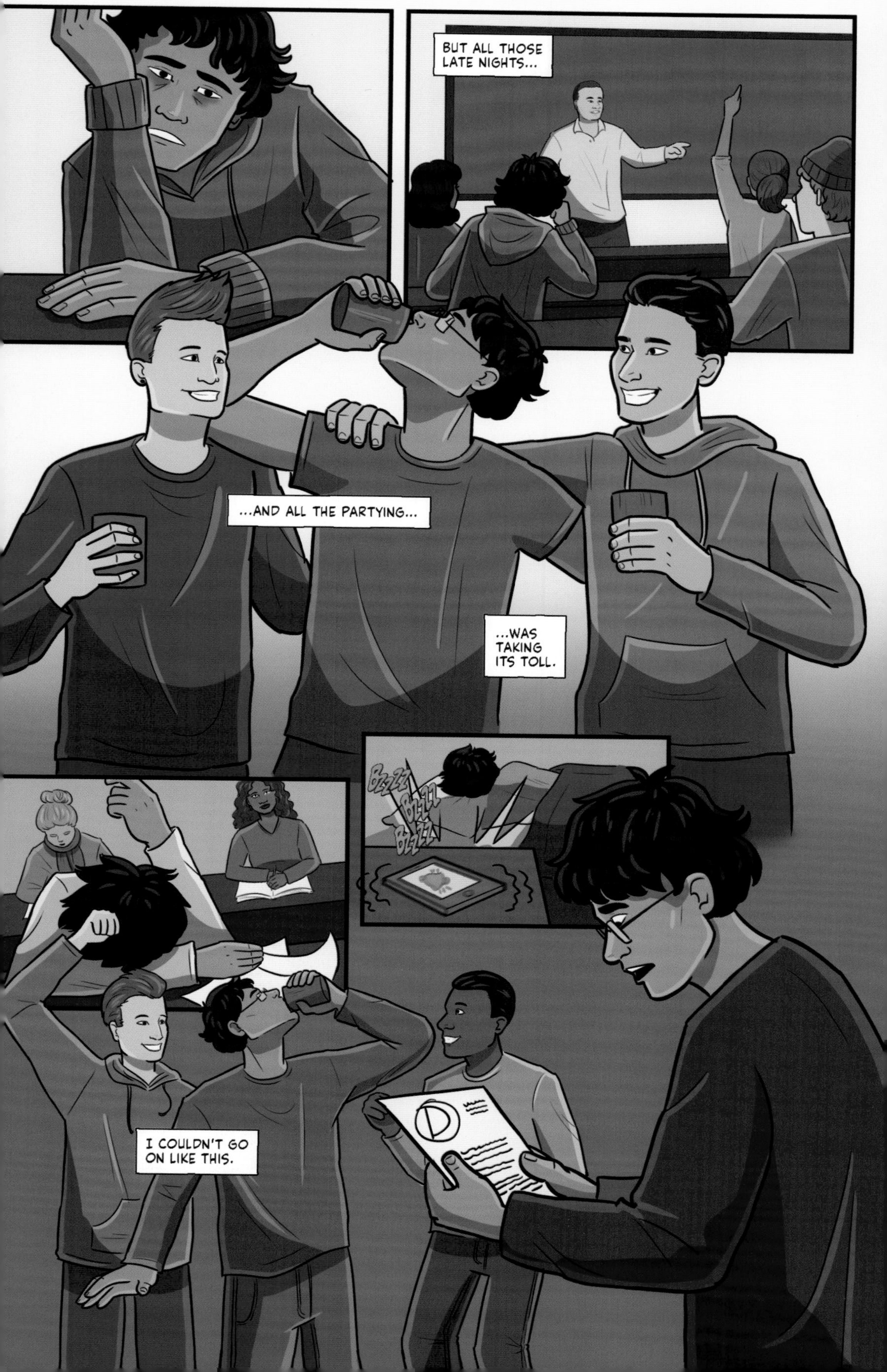

BUT ALL THOSE LATE NIGHTS...
...AND ALL THE PARTYING...
...WAS TAKING ITS TOLL.
Bzzzz Bzzzz Bzzzz
I COULDN'T GO ON LIKE THIS.

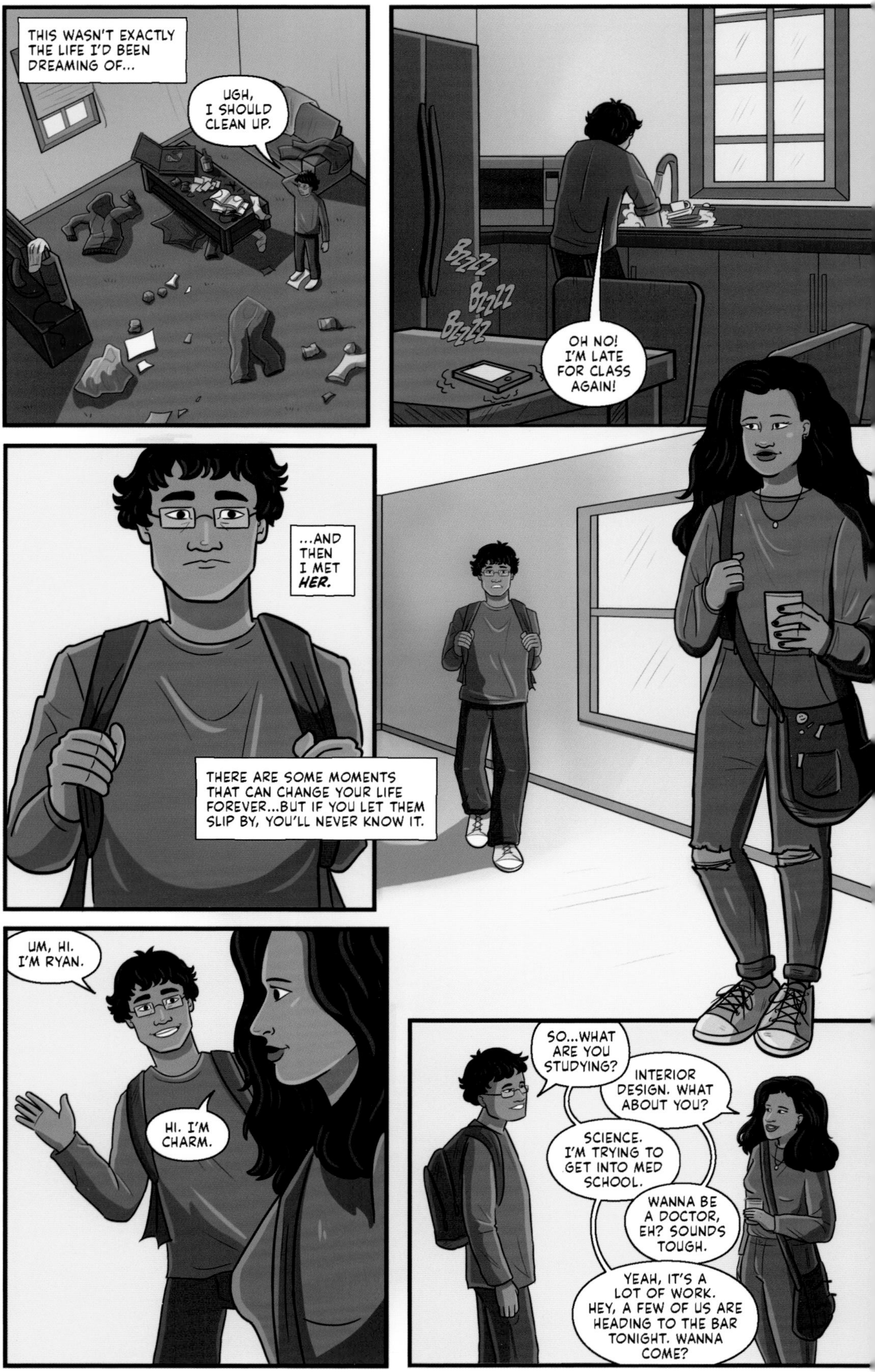
THIS WASN'T EXACTLY THE LIFE I'D BEEN DREAMING OF...
UGH, I SHOULD CLEAN UP.
BZZZZ BZZZZ BZZZZ
OH NO! I'M LATE FOR CLASS AGAIN!
...AND THEN I MET HER.
THERE ARE SOME MOMENTS THAT CAN CHANGE YOUR LIFE FOREVER...BUT IF YOU LET THEM SLIP BY, YOU'LL NEVER KNOW IT.
UM, HI. I'M RYAN.
HI. I'M CHARM.
SO...WHAT ARE YOU STUDYING?
INTERIOR DESIGN. WHAT ABOUT YOU?
SCIENCE. I'M TRYING TO GET INTO MED SCHOOL.
WANNA BE A DOCTOR, EH? SOUNDS TOUGH.
YEAH, IT'S A LOT OF WORK. HEY, A FEW OF US ARE HEADING TO THE BAR TONIGHT. WANNA COME?

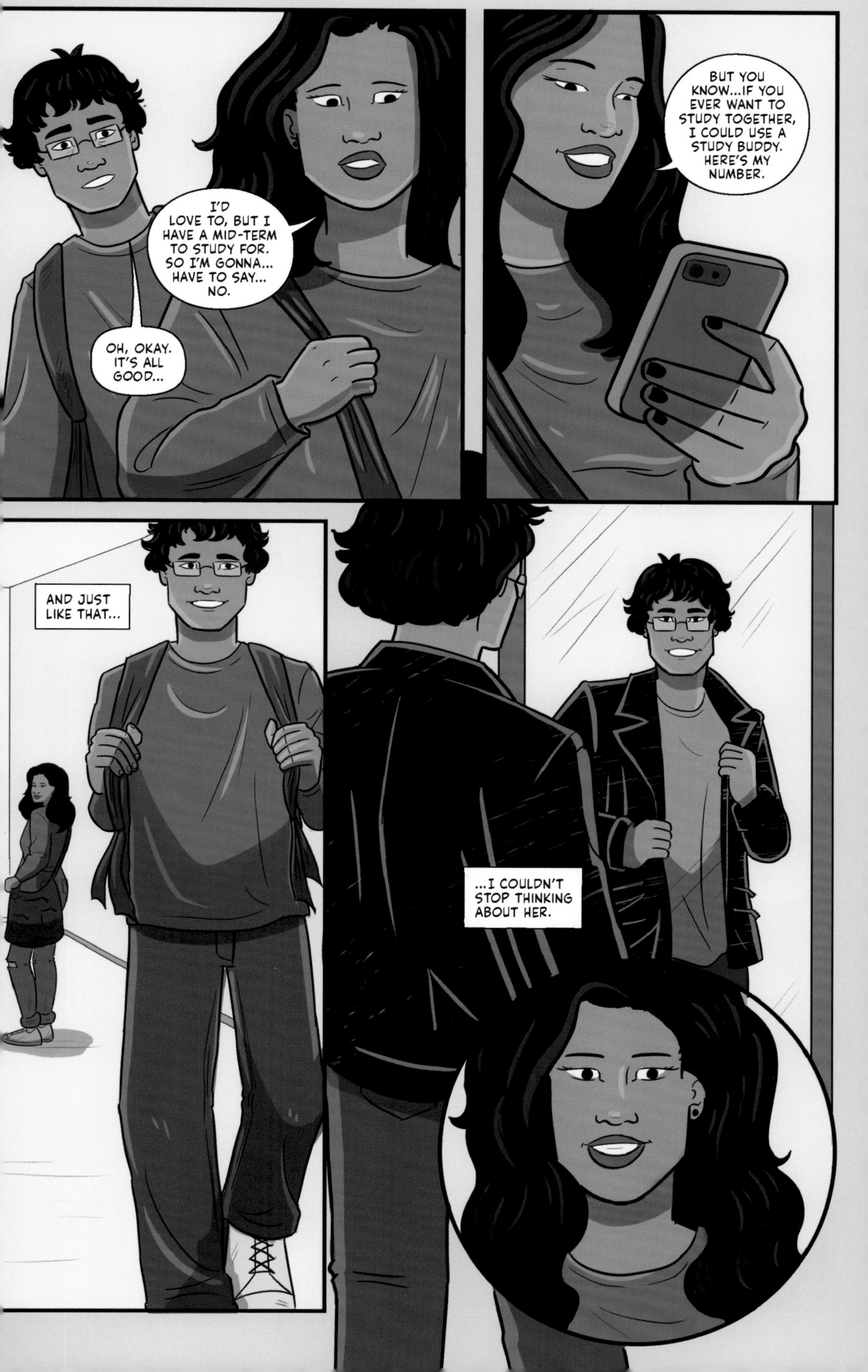
I'D LOVE TO, BUT I HAVE A MID-TERM TO STUDY FOR. SO I'M GONNA... HAVE TO SAY... NO.
OH, OKAY. IT'S ALL GOOD...
BUT YOU KNOW...IF YOU EVER WANT TO STUDY TOGETHER, I COULD USE A STUDY BUDDY. HERE'S MY NUMBER.
AND JUST LIKE THAT...
...I COULDN'T STOP THINKING ABOUT HER.

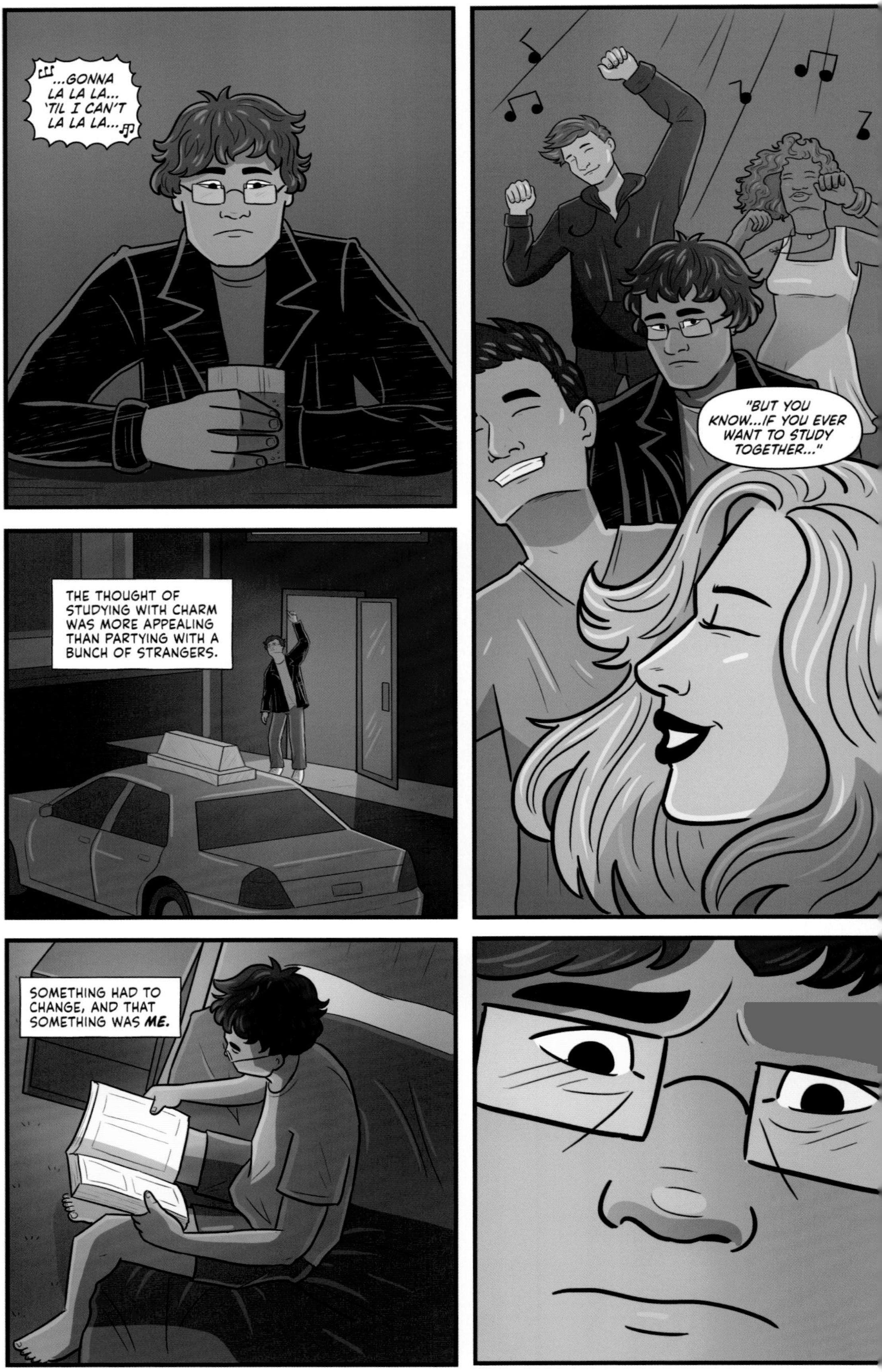
...GONNA LA LA LA... 'TIL I CAN'T LA LA LA...
"BUT YOU KNOW...IF YOU EVER WANT TO STUDY TOGETHER..."
THE THOUGHT OF STUDYING WITH CHARM WAS MORE APPEALING THAN PARTYING WITH A BUNCH OF STRANGERS.
SOMETHING HAD TO CHANGE, AND THAT SOMETHING WAS ***ME.***

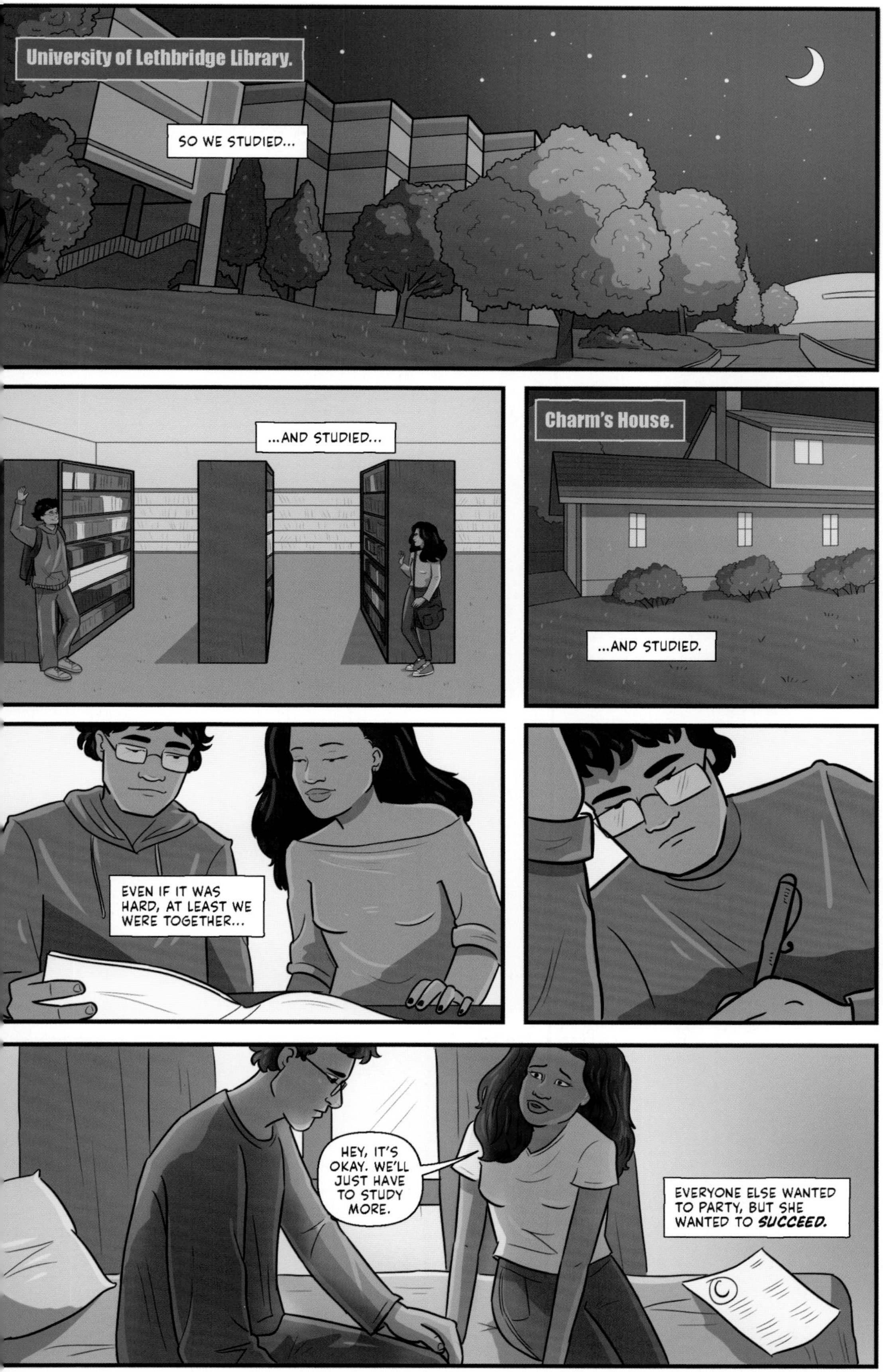
University of Lethbridge Library.
SO WE STUDIED...
...AND STUDIED...
Charm's House.
...AND STUDIED.
EVEN IF IT WAS HARD, AT LEAST WE WERE TOGETHER...
HEY, IT'S OKAY. WE'LL JUST HAVE TO STUDY MORE.
EVERYONE ELSE WANTED TO PARTY, BUT SHE WANTED TO *SUCCEED.*

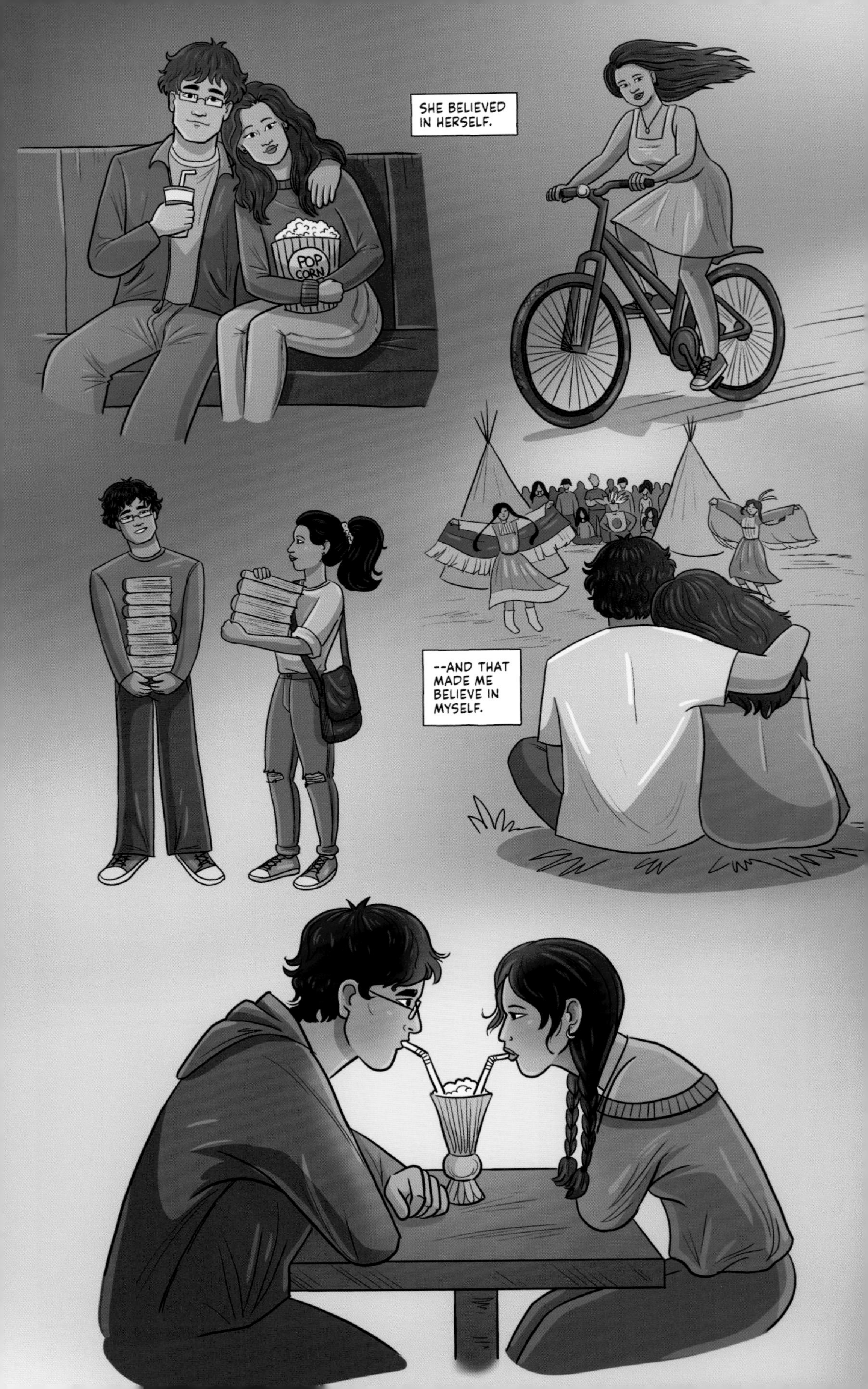
SHE BELIEVED IN HERSELF.
POP CORN
--AND THAT MADE ME BELIEVE IN MYSELF.

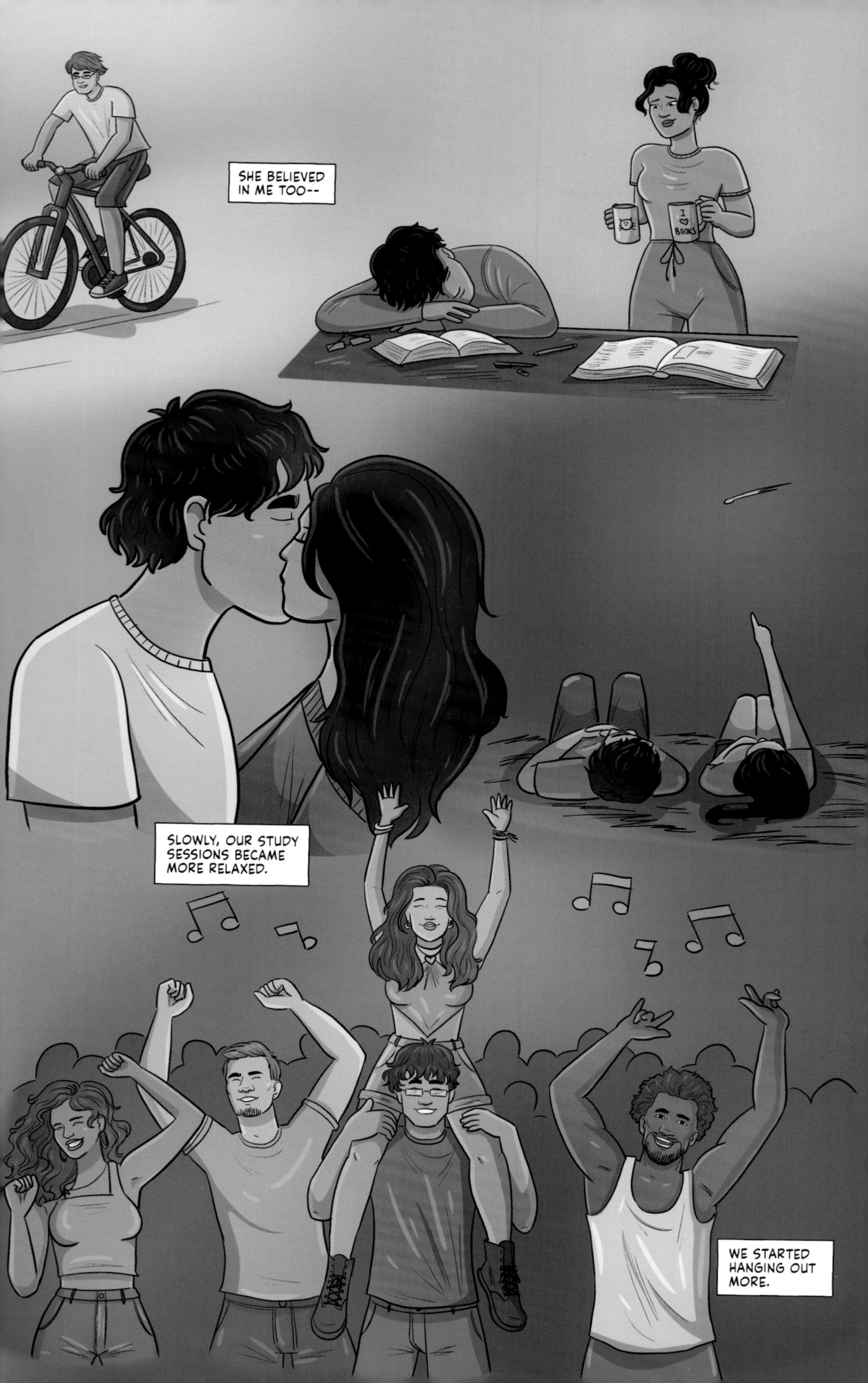
SHE BELIEVED IN ME TOO--
SLOWLY, OUR STUDY SESSIONS BECAME MORE RELAXED.
WE STARTED HANGING OUT MORE.

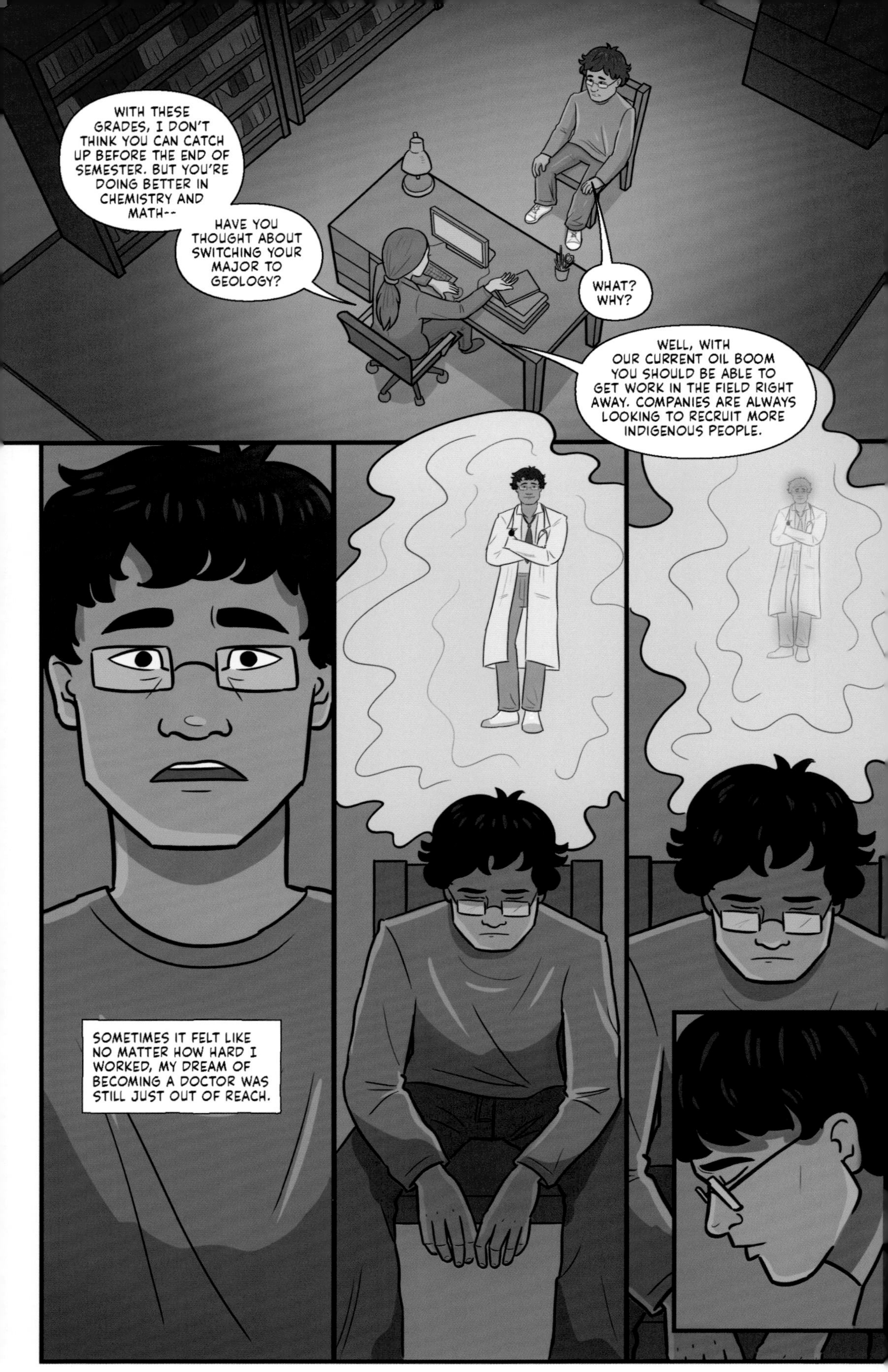
WITH THESE GRADES, I DON'T THINK YOU CAN CATCH UP BEFORE THE END OF SEMESTER. BUT YOU'RE DOING BETTER IN CHEMISTRY AND MATH--
HAVE YOU THOUGHT ABOUT SWITCHING YOUR MAJOR TO GEOLOGY?
WHAT? WHY?
WELL, WITH OUR CURRENT OIL BOOM YOU SHOULD BE ABLE TO GET WORK IN THE FIELD RIGHT AWAY. COMPANIES ARE ALWAYS LOOKING TO RECRUIT MORE INDIGENOUS PEOPLE.
SOMETIMES IT FELT LIKE NO MATTER HOW HARD I WORKED, MY DREAM OF BECOMING A DOCTOR WAS STILL JUST OUT OF REACH.

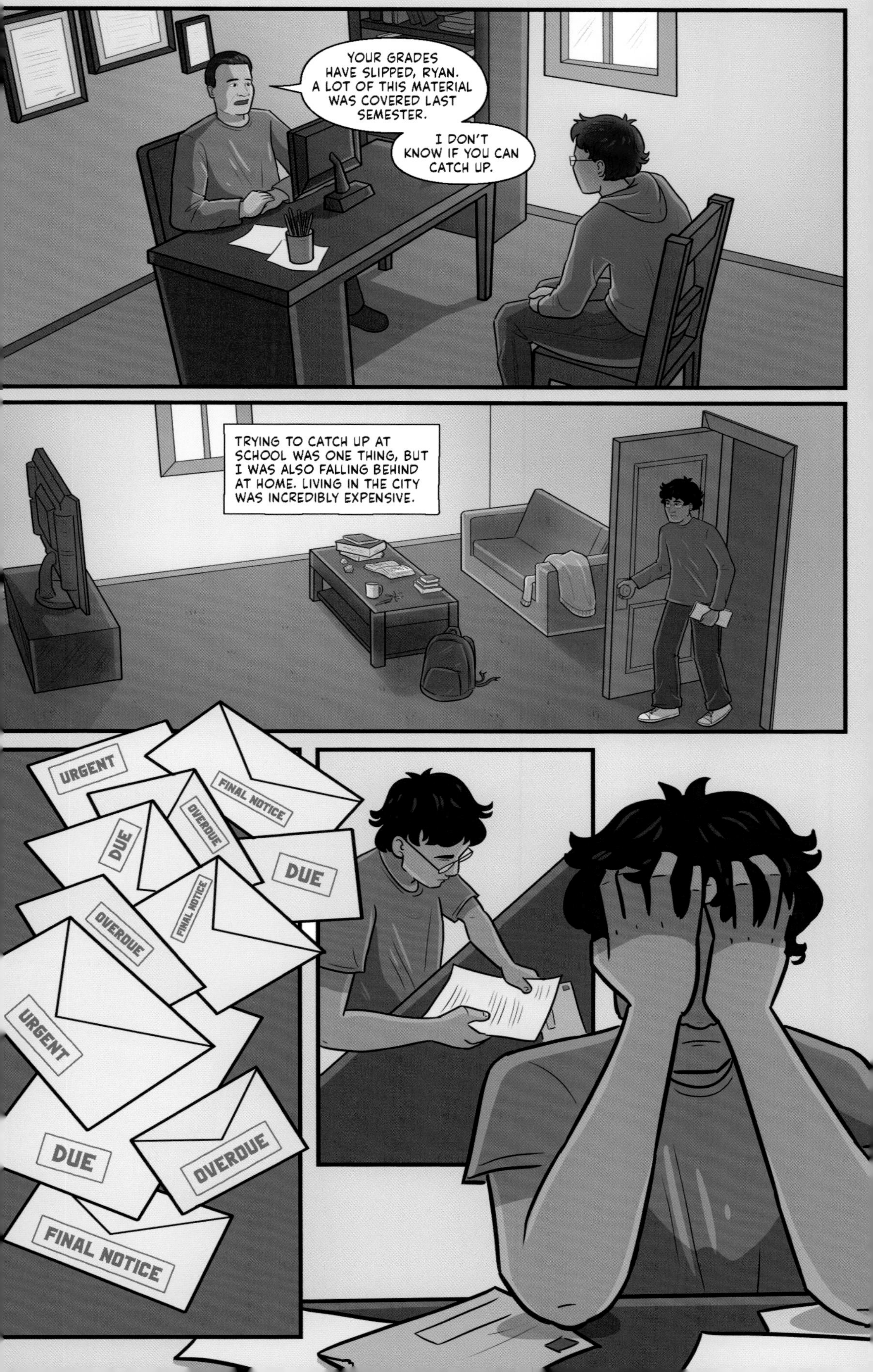
YOUR GRADES HAVE SLIPPED, RYAN. A LOT OF THIS MATERIAL WAS COVERED LAST SEMESTER.
I DON'T KNOW IF YOU CAN CATCH UP.
TRYING TO CATCH UP AT SCHOOL WAS ONE THING, BUT I WAS ALSO FALLING BEHIND AT HOME. LIVING IN THE CITY WAS INCREDIBLY EXPENSIVE.
URGENT
FINAL NOTICE
OVERDUE
DUE
DUE
FINAL NOTICE
OVERDUE
URGENT
DUE
OVERDUE
FINAL NOTICE

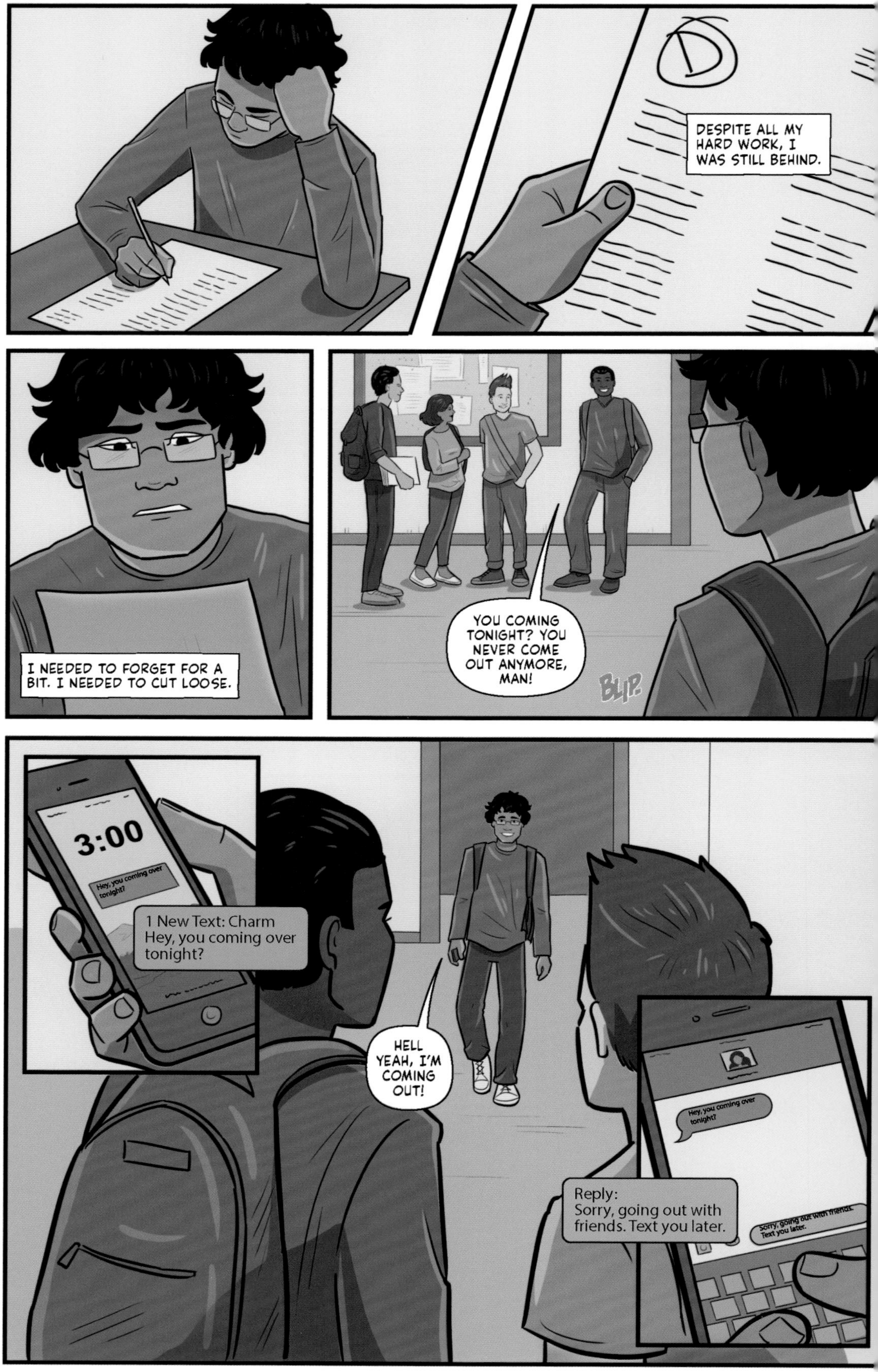
DESPITE ALL MY HARD WORK, I WAS STILL BEHIND.
I NEEDED TO FORGET FOR A BIT. I NEEDED TO CUT LOOSE.
YOU COMING TONIGHT? YOU NEVER COME OUT ANYMORE, MAN!
BLIP.
3:00
Hey, you coming over tonight?
1 New Text: Charm
Hey, you coming over tonight?
HELL YEAH, I'M COMING OUT!
Hey, you coming over tonight?
Reply:
Sorry, going out with friends. Text you later.
Sorry, going out with friends. Text you later.

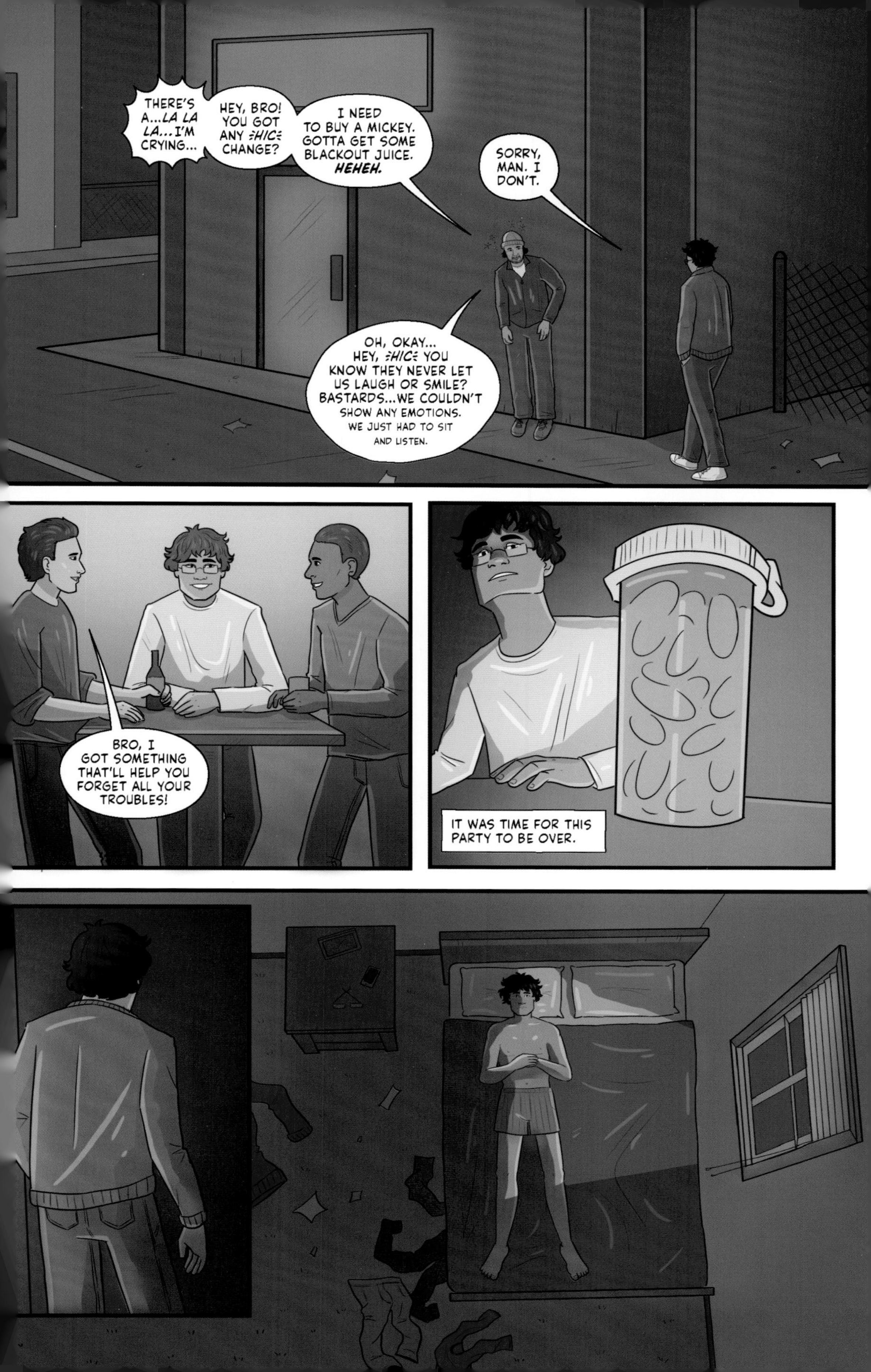
THERE'S A...LA LA LA...I'M CRYING...
HEY, BRO! YOU GOT ANY HIC CHANGE?
I NEED TO BUY A MICKEY. GOTTA GET SOME BLACKOUT JUICE. HEHEH.
SORRY, MAN. I DON'T.
OH, OKAY... HEY, HIC YOU KNOW THEY NEVER LET US LAUGH OR SMILE? BASTARDS...WE COULDN'T SHOW ANY EMOTIONS. WE JUST HAD TO SIT AND LISTEN.
BRO, I GOT SOMETHING THAT'LL HELP YOU FORGET ALL YOUR TROUBLES!
IT WAS TIME FOR THIS PARTY TO BE OVER.

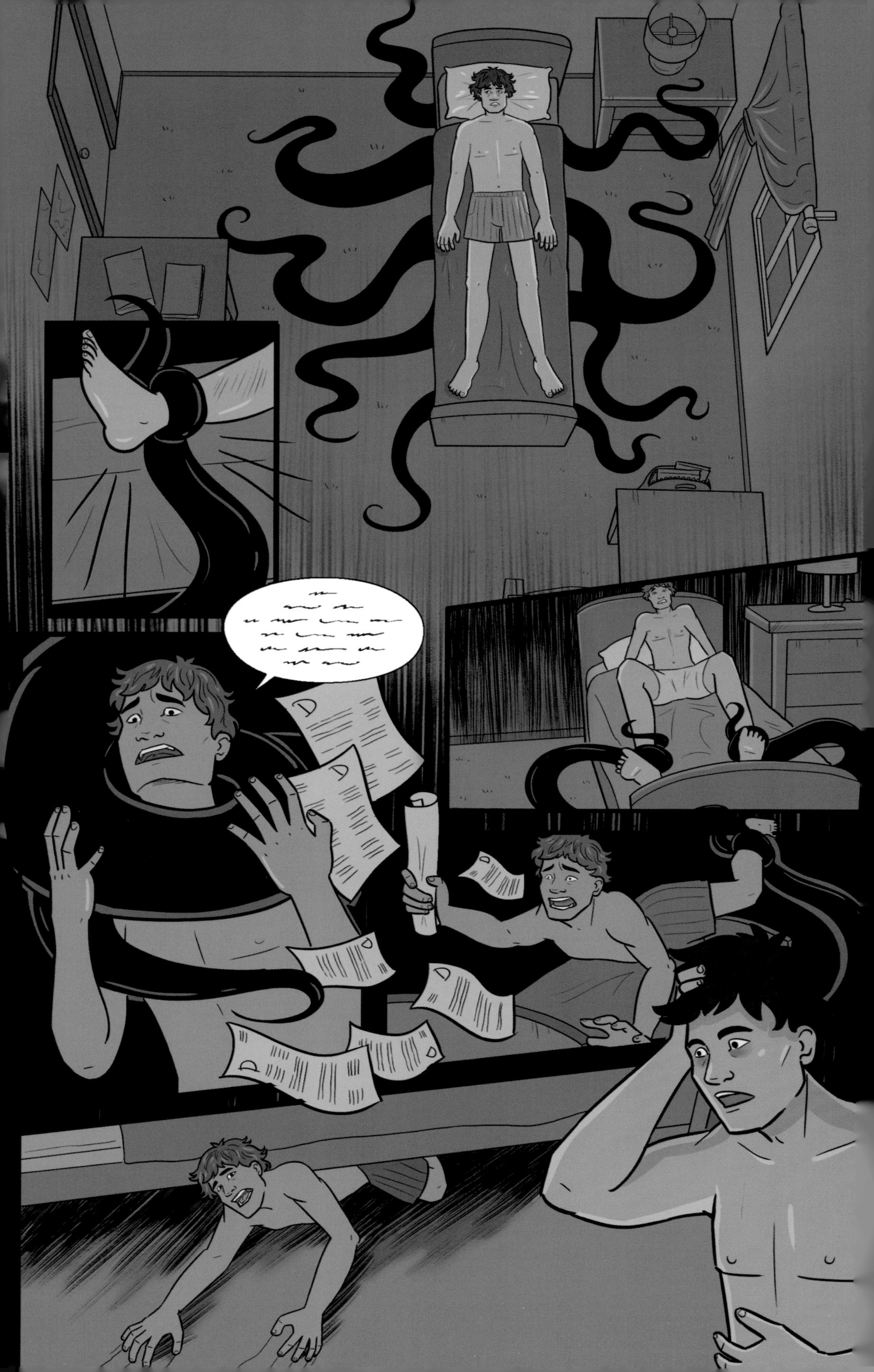

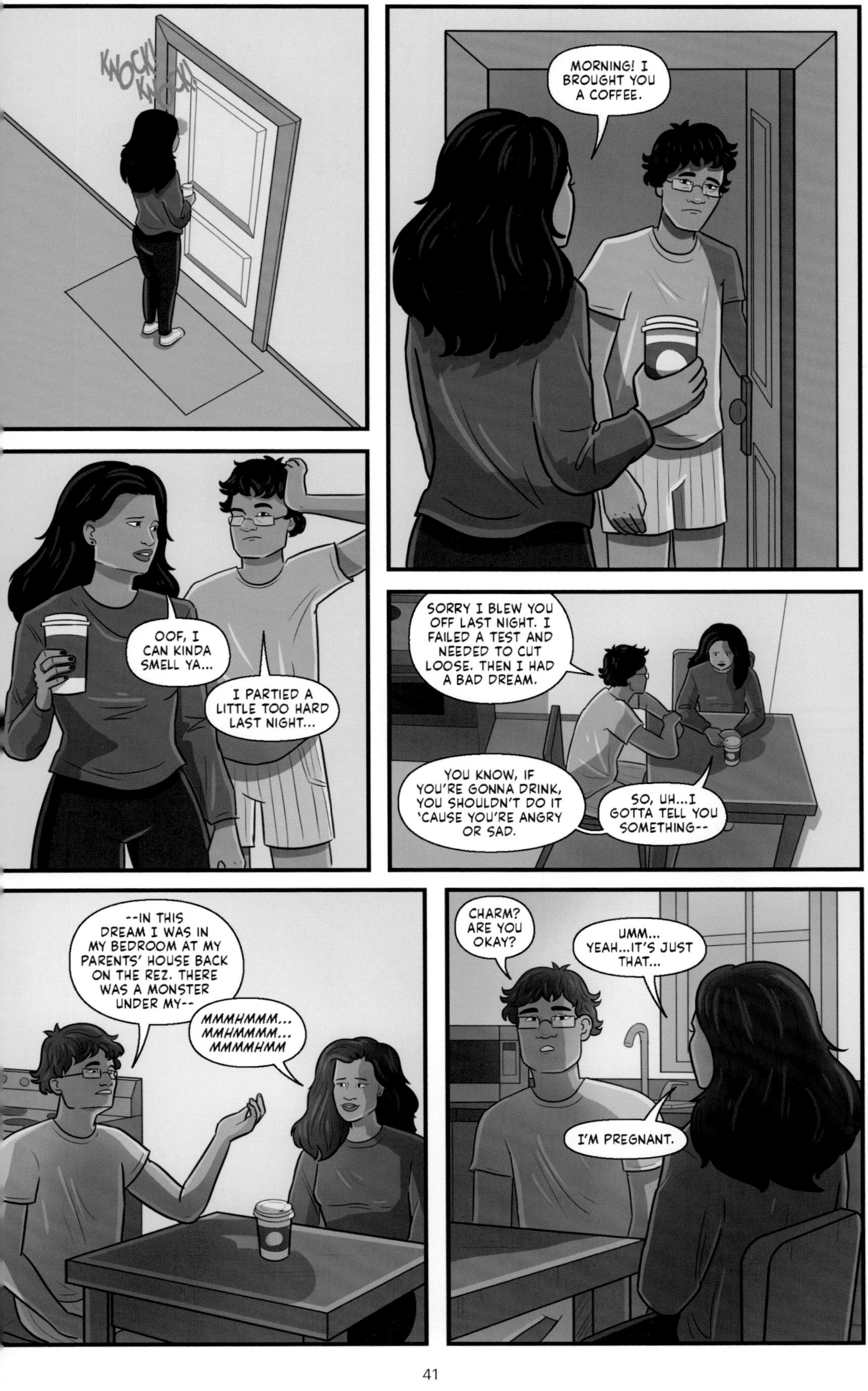
KNOCK! KNOCK!
MORNING! I BROUGHT YOU A COFFEE.
OOF, I CAN KINDA SMELL YA...
I PARTIED A LITTLE TOO HARD LAST NIGHT...
SORRY I BLEW YOU OFF LAST NIGHT. I FAILED A TEST AND NEEDED TO CUT LOOSE. THEN I HAD A BAD DREAM.
YOU KNOW, IF YOU'RE GONNA DRINK, YOU SHOULDN'T DO IT 'CAUSE YOU'RE ANGRY OR SAD.
SO, UH...I GOTTA TELL YOU SOMETHING--
--IN THIS DREAM I WAS IN MY BEDROOM AT MY PARENTS' HOUSE BACK ON THE REZ. THERE WAS A MONSTER UNDER MY--
MMMHMMM... MMHMMMM... MMMMHMM
CHARM? ARE YOU OKAY?
UMM... YEAH...IT'S JUST THAT...
I'M PREGNANT.

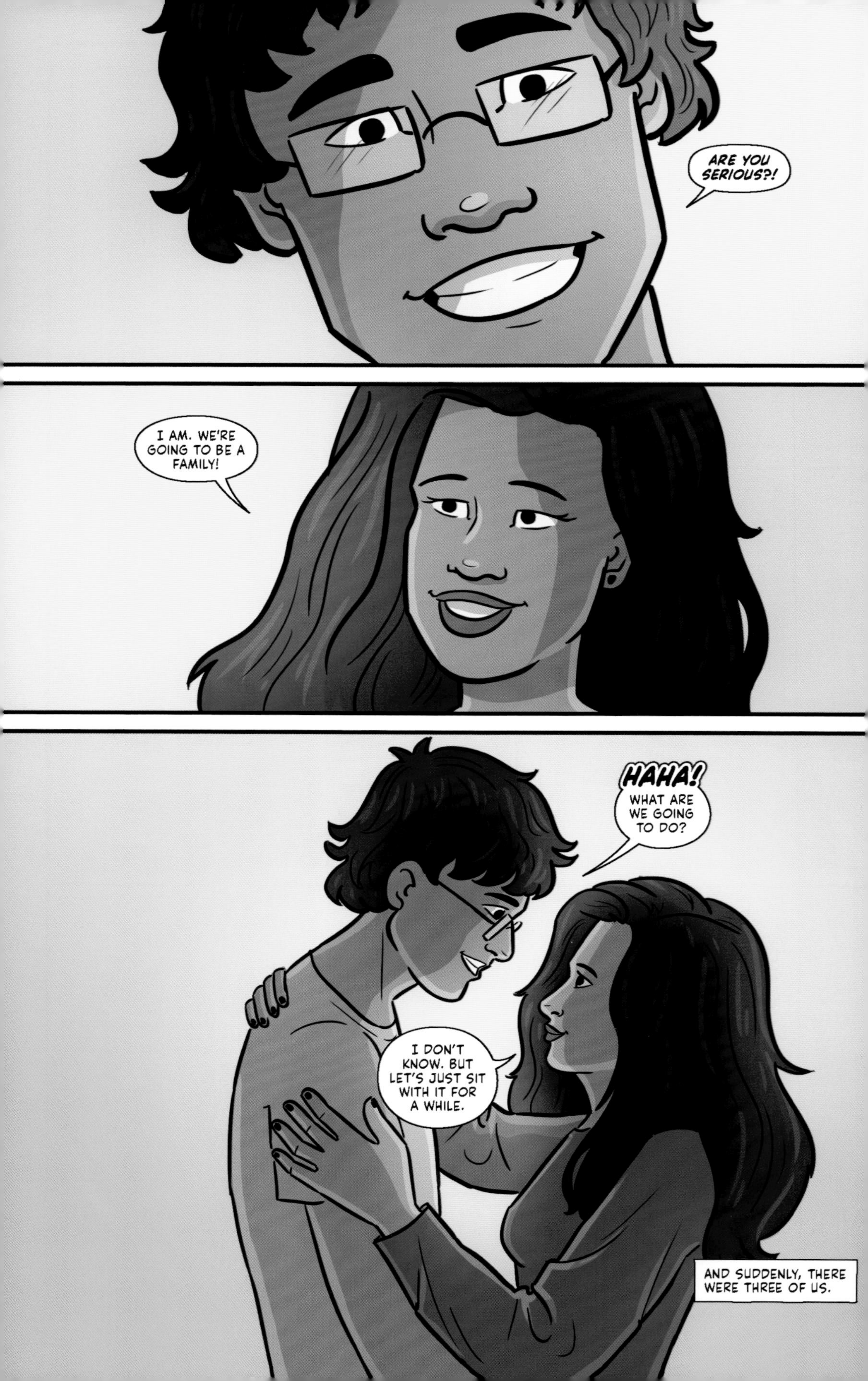
ARE YOU SERIOUS?!
I AM. WE'RE GOING TO BE A FAMILY!
HAHA!
WHAT ARE WE GOING TO DO?
I DON'T KNOW. BUT LET'S JUST SIT WITH IT FOR A WHILE.
AND SUDDENLY, THERE WERE THREE OF US.

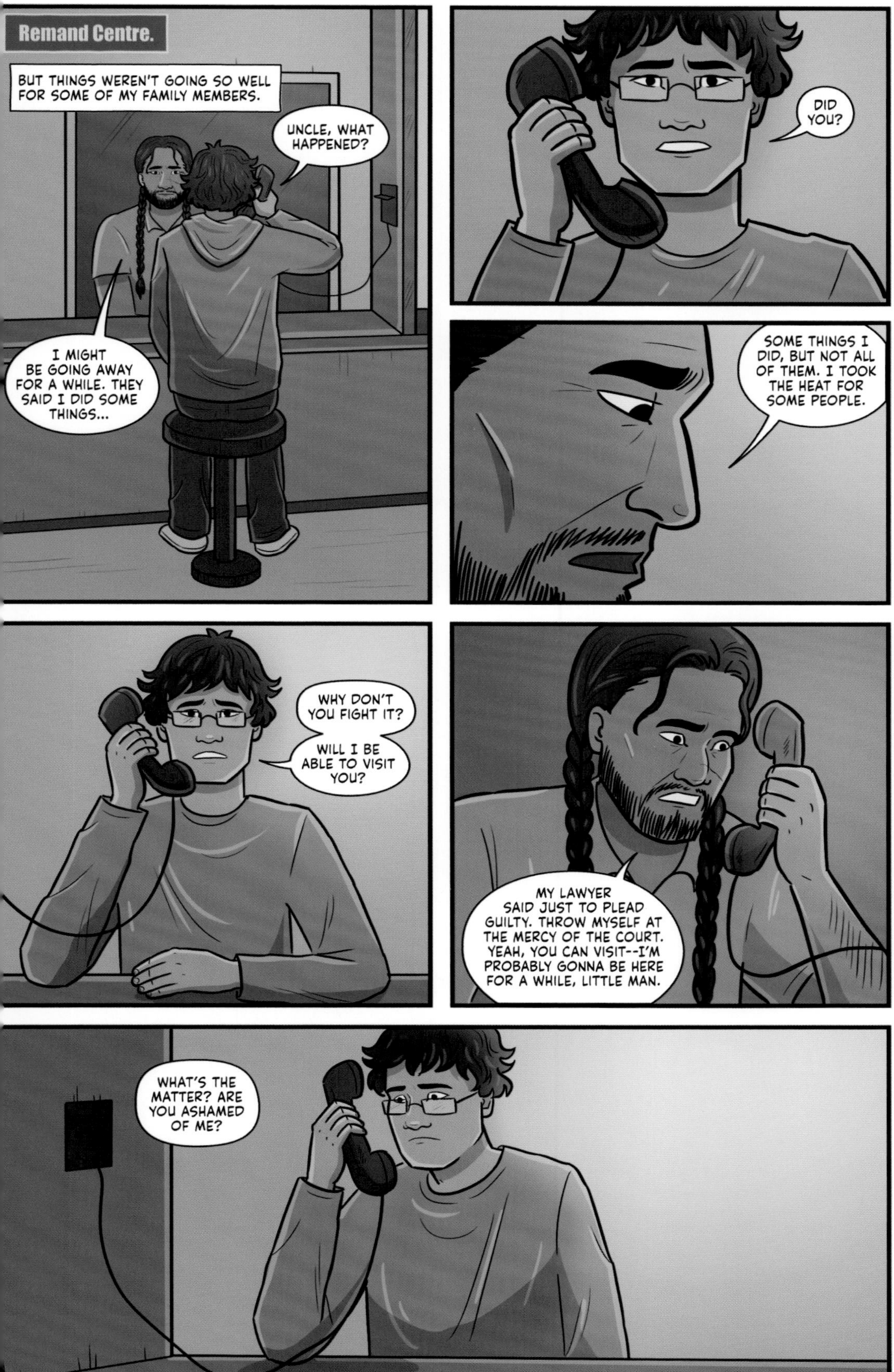
Remand Centre.
BUT THINGS WEREN'T GOING SO WELL FOR SOME OF MY FAMILY MEMBERS.
UNCLE, WHAT HAPPENED?
I MIGHT BE GOING AWAY FOR A WHILE. THEY SAID I DID SOME THINGS...
DID YOU?
SOME THINGS I DID, BUT NOT ALL OF THEM. I TOOK THE HEAT FOR SOME PEOPLE.
WHY DON'T YOU FIGHT IT?
WILL I BE ABLE TO VISIT YOU?
MY LAWYER SAID JUST TO PLEAD GUILTY. THROW MYSELF AT THE MERCY OF THE COURT. YEAH, YOU CAN VISIT--I'M PROBABLY GONNA BE HERE FOR A WHILE, LITTLE MAN.
WHAT'S THE MATTER? ARE YOU ASHAMED OF ME?

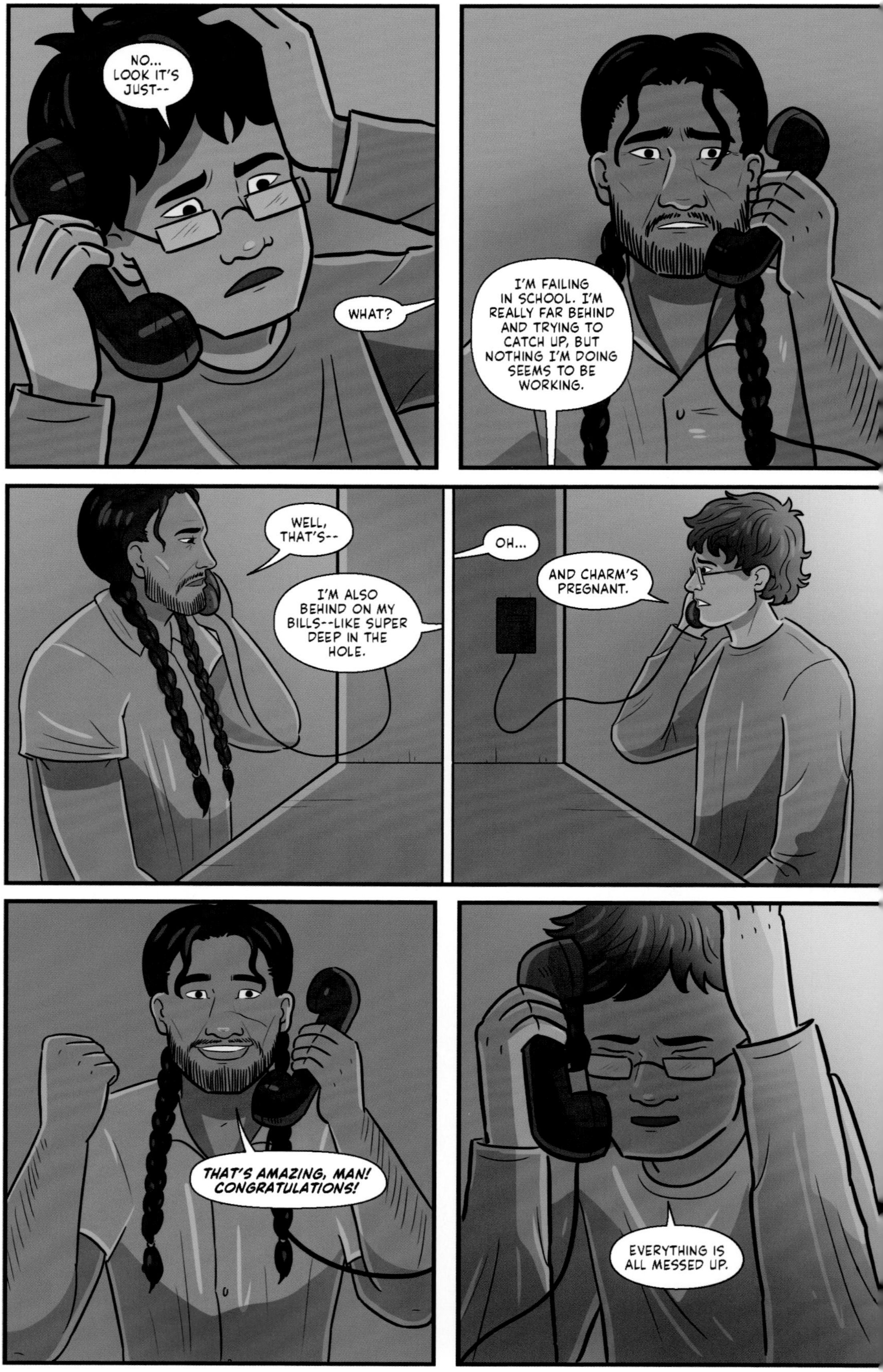
NO... LOOK IT'S JUST--
WHAT?
I'M FAILING IN SCHOOL. I'M REALLY FAR BEHIND AND TRYING TO CATCH UP, BUT NOTHING I'M DOING SEEMS TO BE WORKING.
WELL, THAT'S--
I'M ALSO BEHIND ON MY BILLS--LIKE SUPER DEEP IN THE HOLE.
OH...
AND CHARM'S PREGNANT.
THAT'S AMAZING, MAN! CONGRATULATIONS!
EVERYTHING IS ALL MESSED UP.

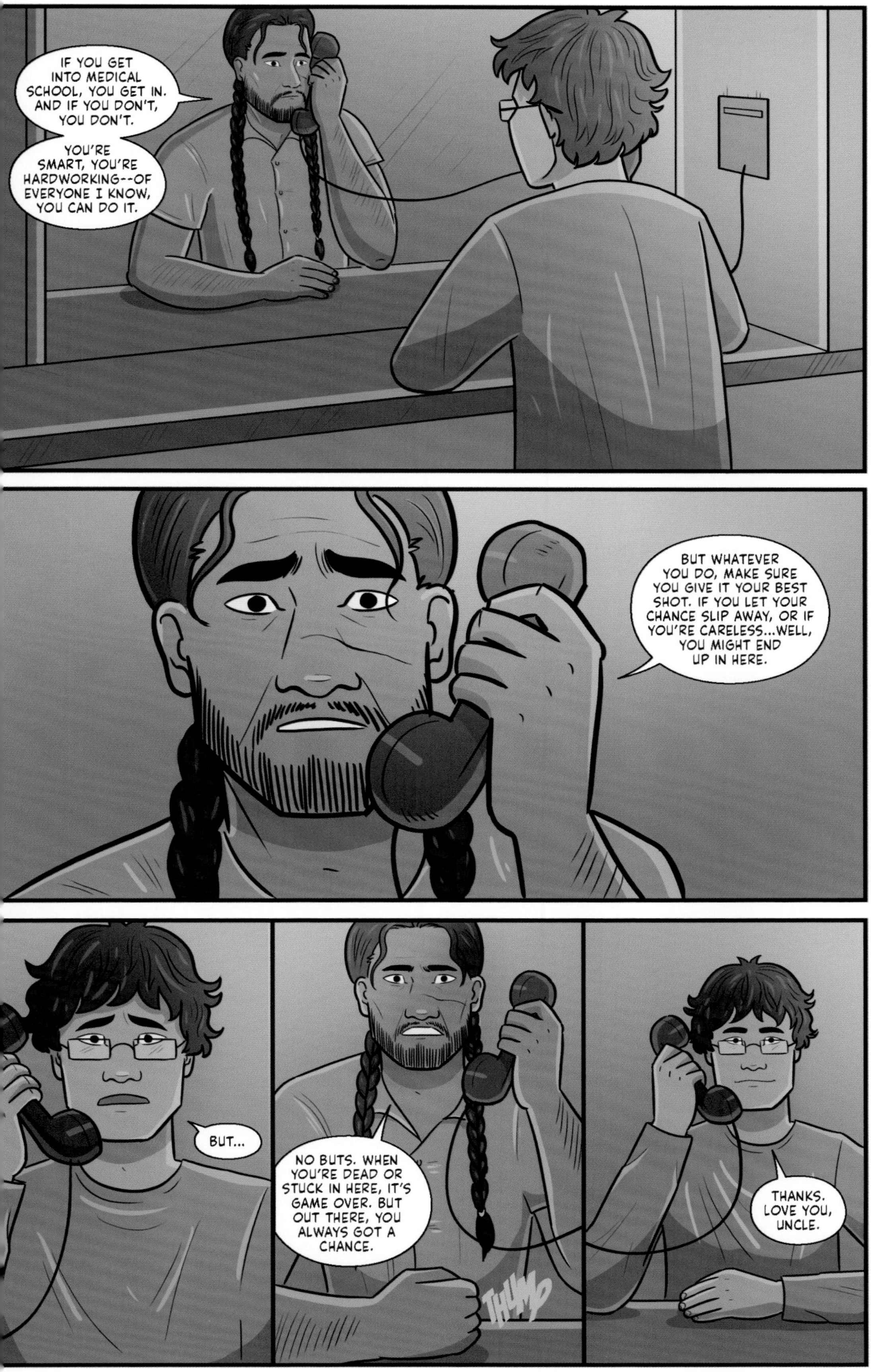
IF YOU GET INTO MEDICAL SCHOOL, YOU GET IN. AND IF YOU DON'T, YOU DON'T.
YOU'RE SMART, YOU'RE HARDWORKING--OF EVERYONE I KNOW, YOU CAN DO IT.
BUT WHATEVER YOU DO, MAKE SURE YOU GIVE IT YOUR BEST SHOT. IF YOU LET YOUR CHANCE SLIP AWAY, OR IF YOU'RE CARELESS...WELL, YOU MIGHT END UP IN HERE.
BUT...
NO BUTS. WHEN YOU'RE DEAD OR STUCK IN HERE, IT'S GAME OVER. BUT OUT THERE, YOU ALWAYS GOT A CHANCE.
THUMP
THANKS. LOVE YOU, UNCLE.

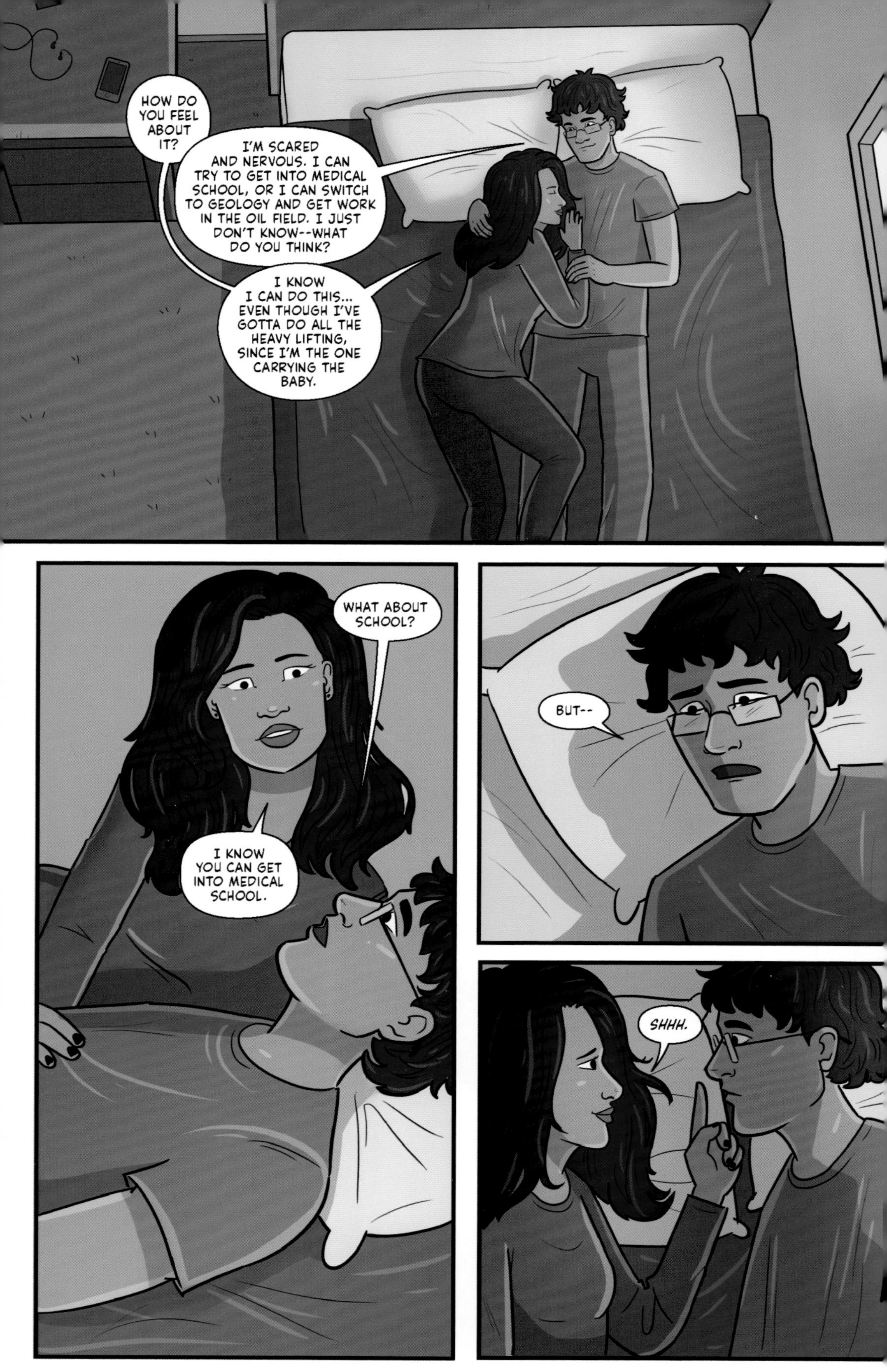
HOW DO YOU FEEL ABOUT IT?
I'M SCARED AND NERVOUS. I CAN TRY TO GET INTO MEDICAL SCHOOL, OR I CAN SWITCH TO GEOLOGY AND GET WORK IN THE OIL FIELD. I JUST DON'T KNOW--WHAT DO YOU THINK?
I KNOW I CAN DO THIS... EVEN THOUGH I'VE GOTTA DO ALL THE HEAVY LIFTING, SINCE I'M THE ONE CARRYING THE BABY.
WHAT ABOUT SCHOOL?
I KNOW YOU CAN GET INTO MEDICAL SCHOOL.
BUT--
SHHH.

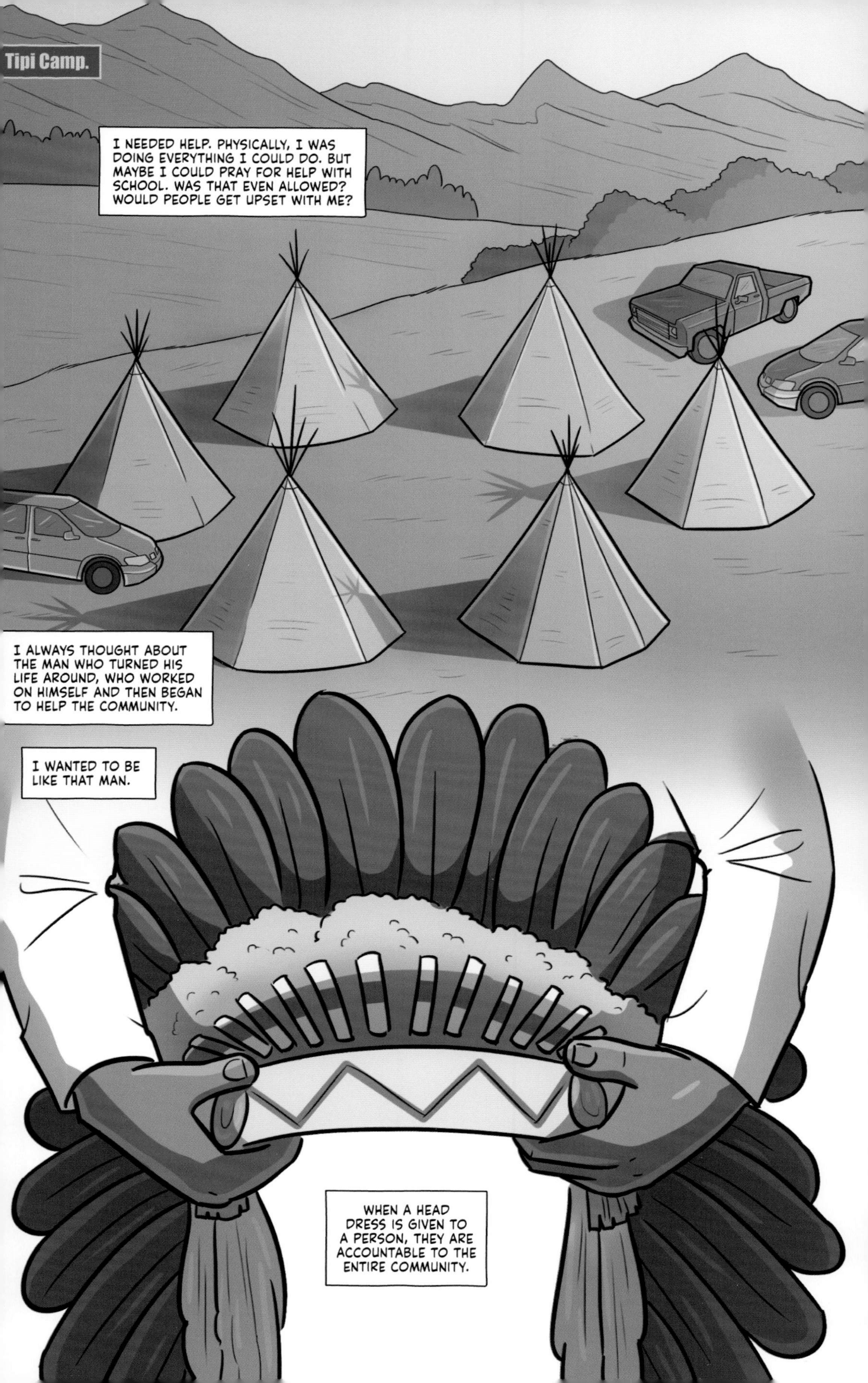
Tipi Camp.
I NEEDED HELP. PHYSICALLY, I WAS DOING EVERYTHING I COULD DO. BUT MAYBE I COULD PRAY FOR HELP WITH SCHOOL. WAS THAT EVEN ALLOWED? WOULD PEOPLE GET UPSET WITH ME?
I ALWAYS THOUGHT ABOUT THE MAN WHO TURNED HIS LIFE AROUND, WHO WORKED ON HIMSELF AND THEN BEGAN TO HELP THE COMMUNITY.
I WANTED TO BE LIKE THAT MAN.
WHEN A HEAD DRESS IS GIVEN TO A PERSON, THEY ARE ACCOUNTABLE TO THE ENTIRE COMMUNITY.

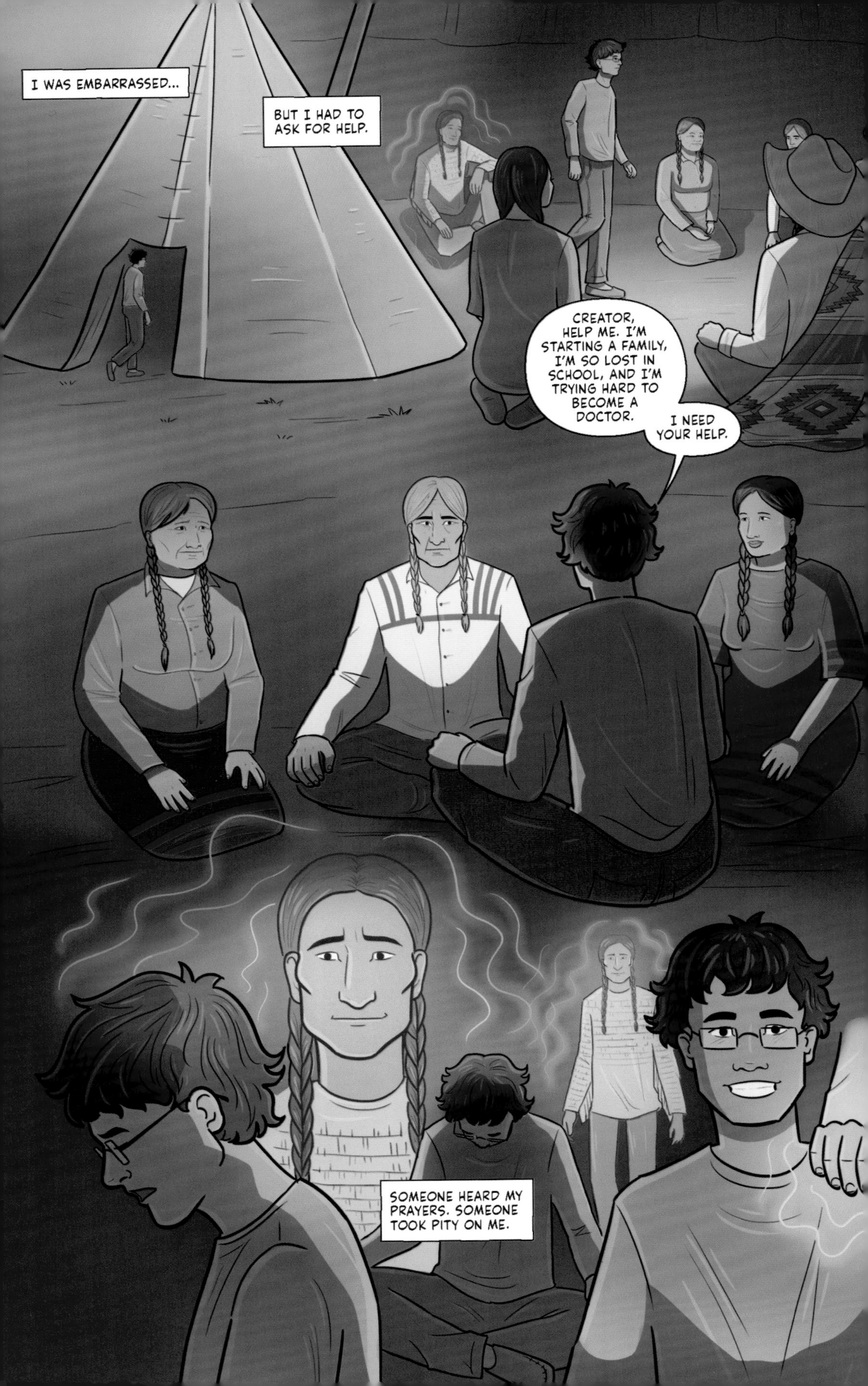
I WAS EMBARRASSED...
BUT I HAD TO ASK FOR HELP.
CREATOR, HELP ME. I'M STARTING A FAMILY, I'M SO LOST IN SCHOOL, AND I'M TRYING HARD TO BECOME A DOCTOR.
I NEED YOUR HELP.
SOMEONE HEARD MY PRAYERS. SOMEONE TOOK PITY ON ME.

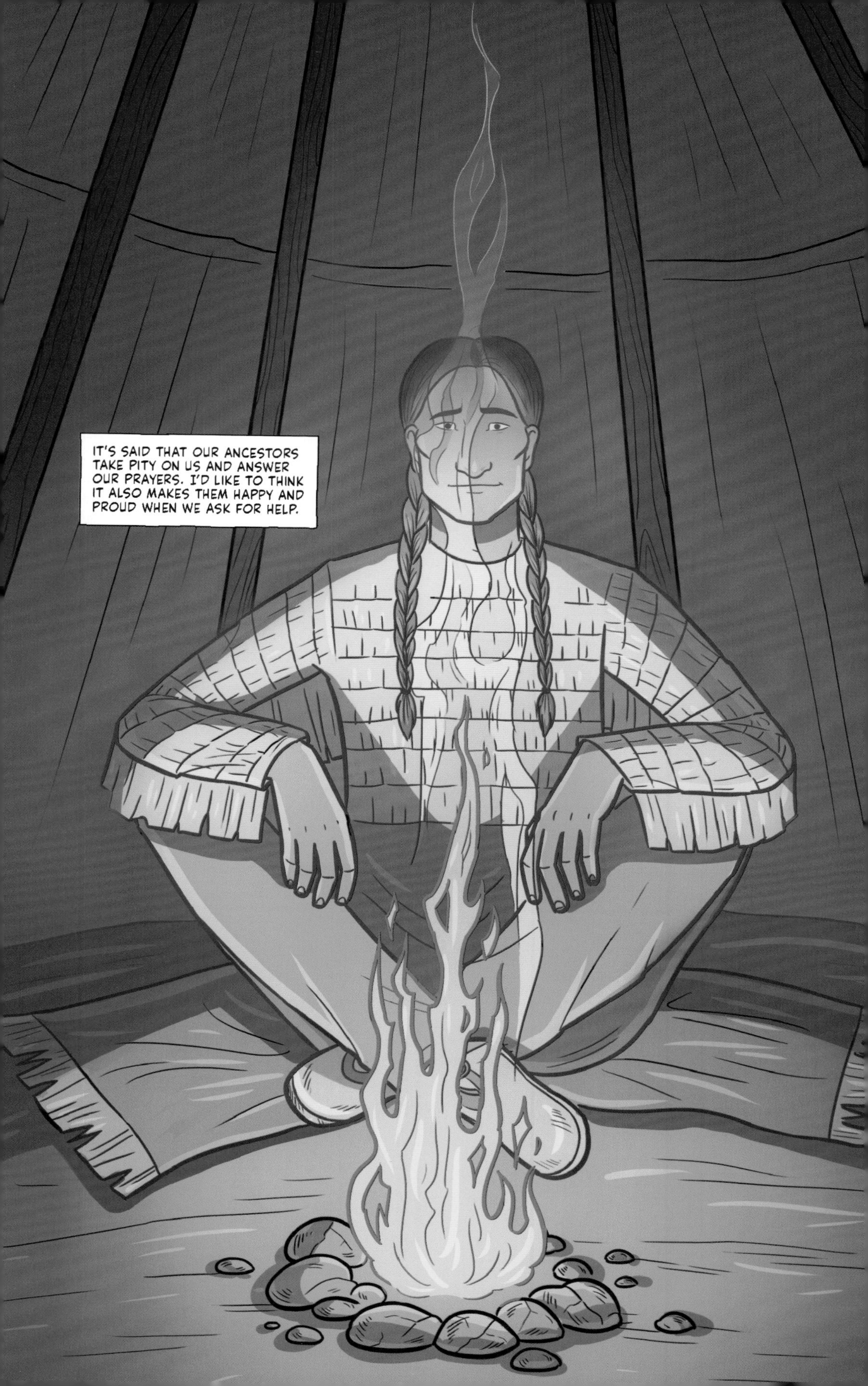
IT'S SAID THAT OUR ANCESTORS TAKE PITY ON US AND ANSWER OUR PRAYERS. I'D LIKE TO THINK IT ALSO MAKES THEM HAPPY AND PROUD WHEN WE ASK FOR HELP.

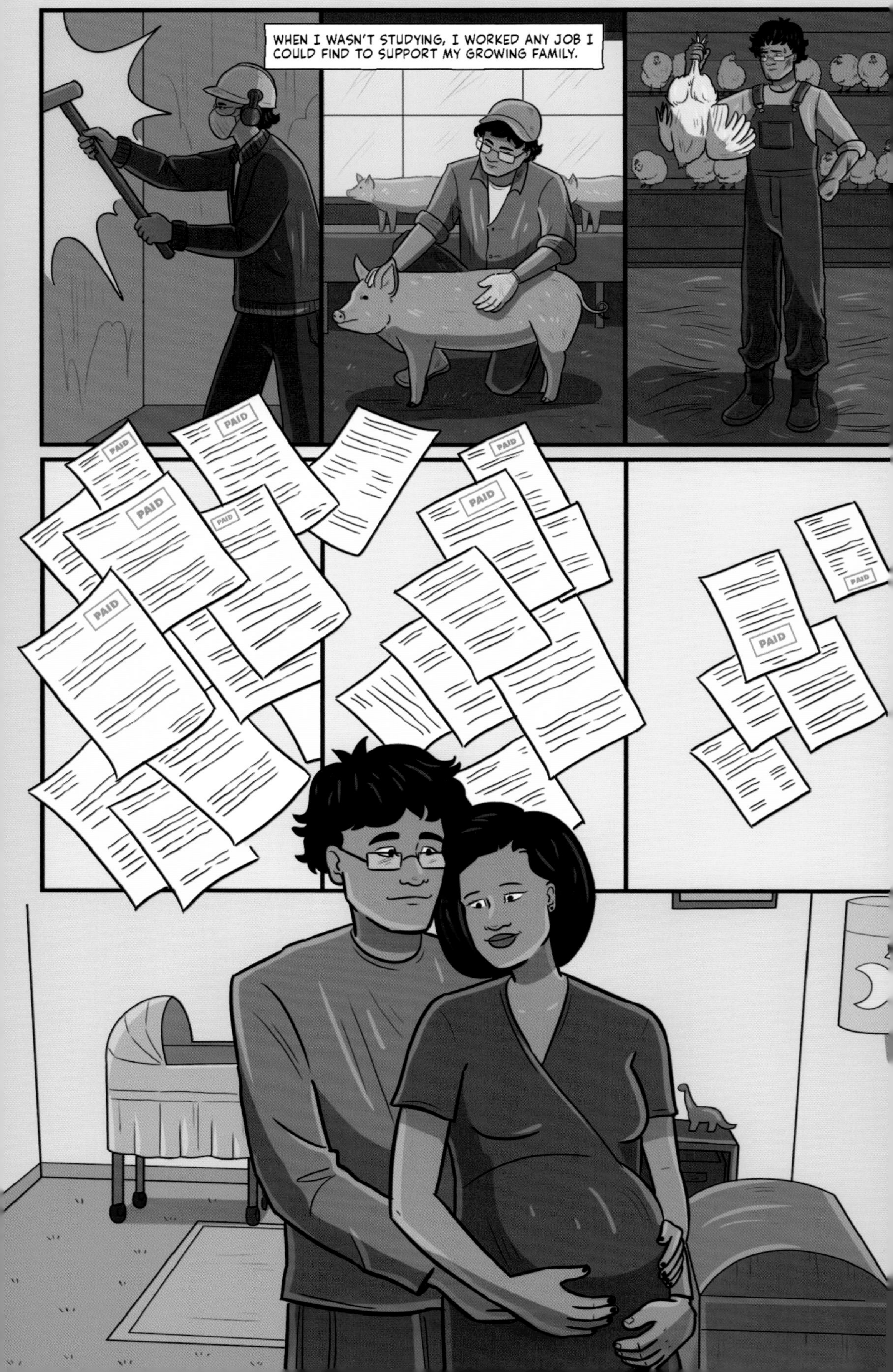
WHEN I WASN'T STUDYING, I WORKED ANY JOB I COULD FIND TO SUPPORT MY GROWING FAMILY.
PAID
PAID
PAID
PAID
PAID
PAID
PAID
PAID
PAID

EVEN WITH ALL MY SCIENTIFIC KNOWLEDGE...

...NOTHING QUITE PREPARED ME FOR BECOMING A PARENT.

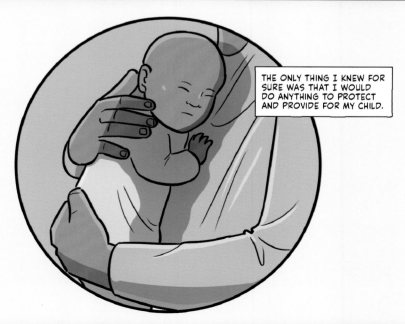

THE ONLY THING I KNEW FOR SURE WAS THAT I WOULD DO ANYTHING TO PROTECT AND PROVIDE FOR MY CHILD.

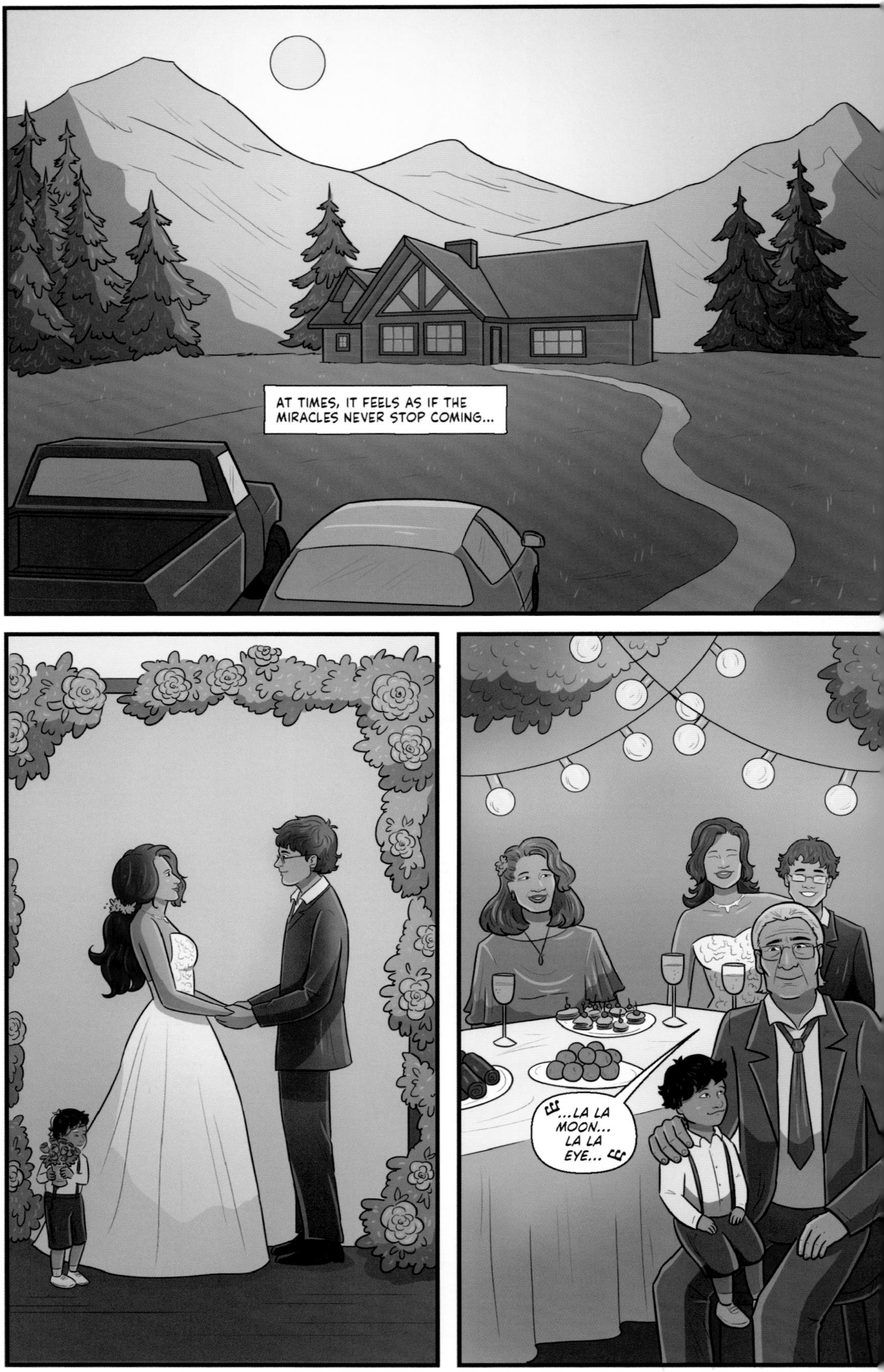
AT TIMES, IT FEELS AS IF THE MIRACLES NEVER STOP COMING...
...LA LA MOON... LA LA EYE...

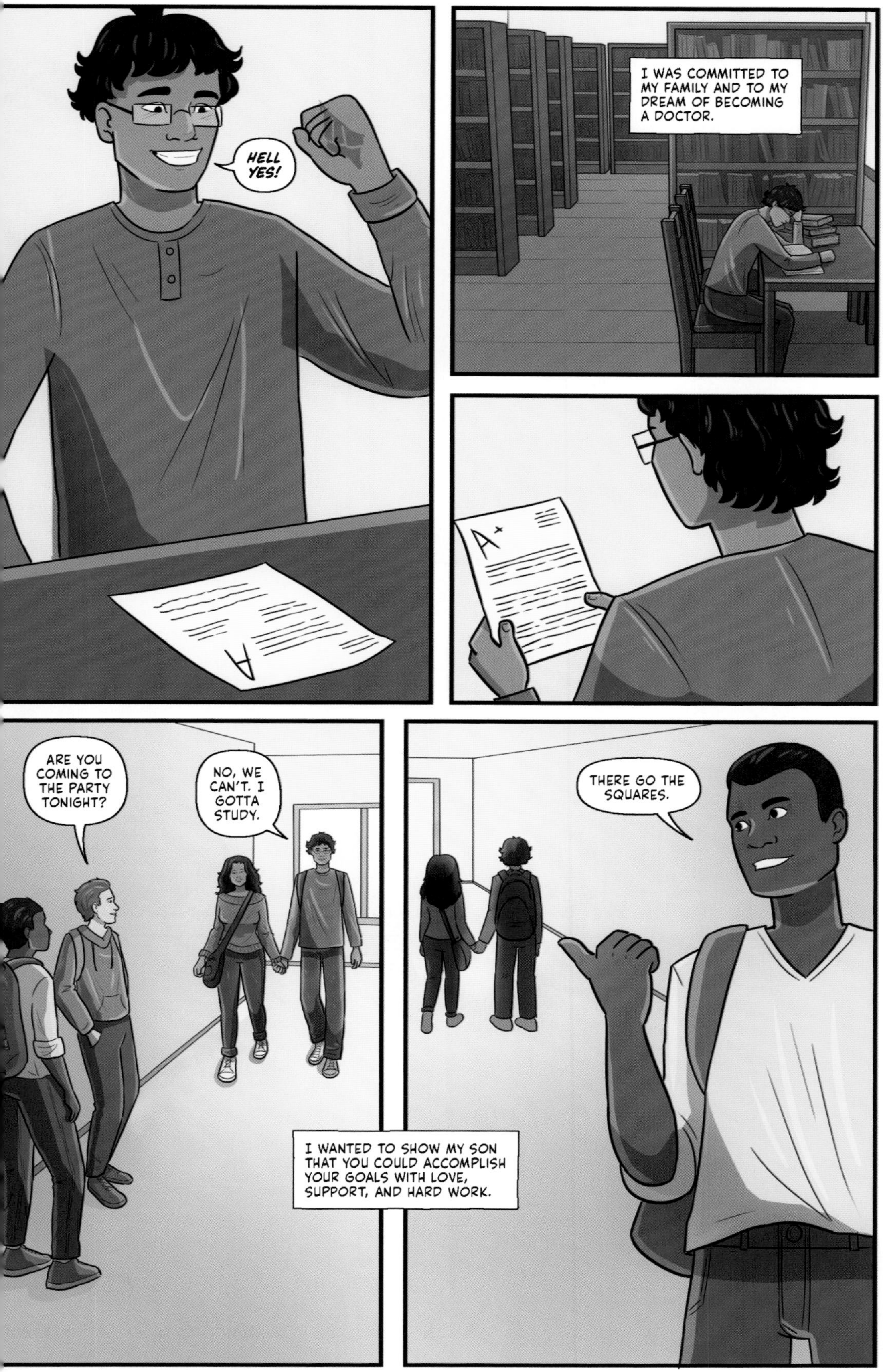
HELL YES!
I WAS COMMITTED TO MY FAMILY AND TO MY DREAM OF BECOMING A DOCTOR.
ARE YOU COMING TO THE PARTY TONIGHT?
NO, WE CAN'T. I GOTTA STUDY.
THERE GO THE SQUARES.
I WANTED TO SHOW MY SON THAT YOU COULD ACCOMPLISH YOUR GOALS WITH LOVE, SUPPORT, AND HARD WORK.

SO, WHEN THE DAY FINALLY CAME...

Faculty of Medicine and Dentistry

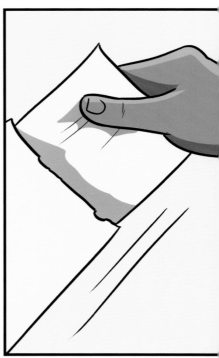

Dear Mr. Fox,

Congratulations!

It is with great pleasure that I write to inform you that you have been admitted to the Medical Sciences program at the University of Alberta.

I'M GOING TO MED SCHOOL!

...I CELEBRATED MY FAMILY'S SUCCESS, NOT JUST MY OWN.

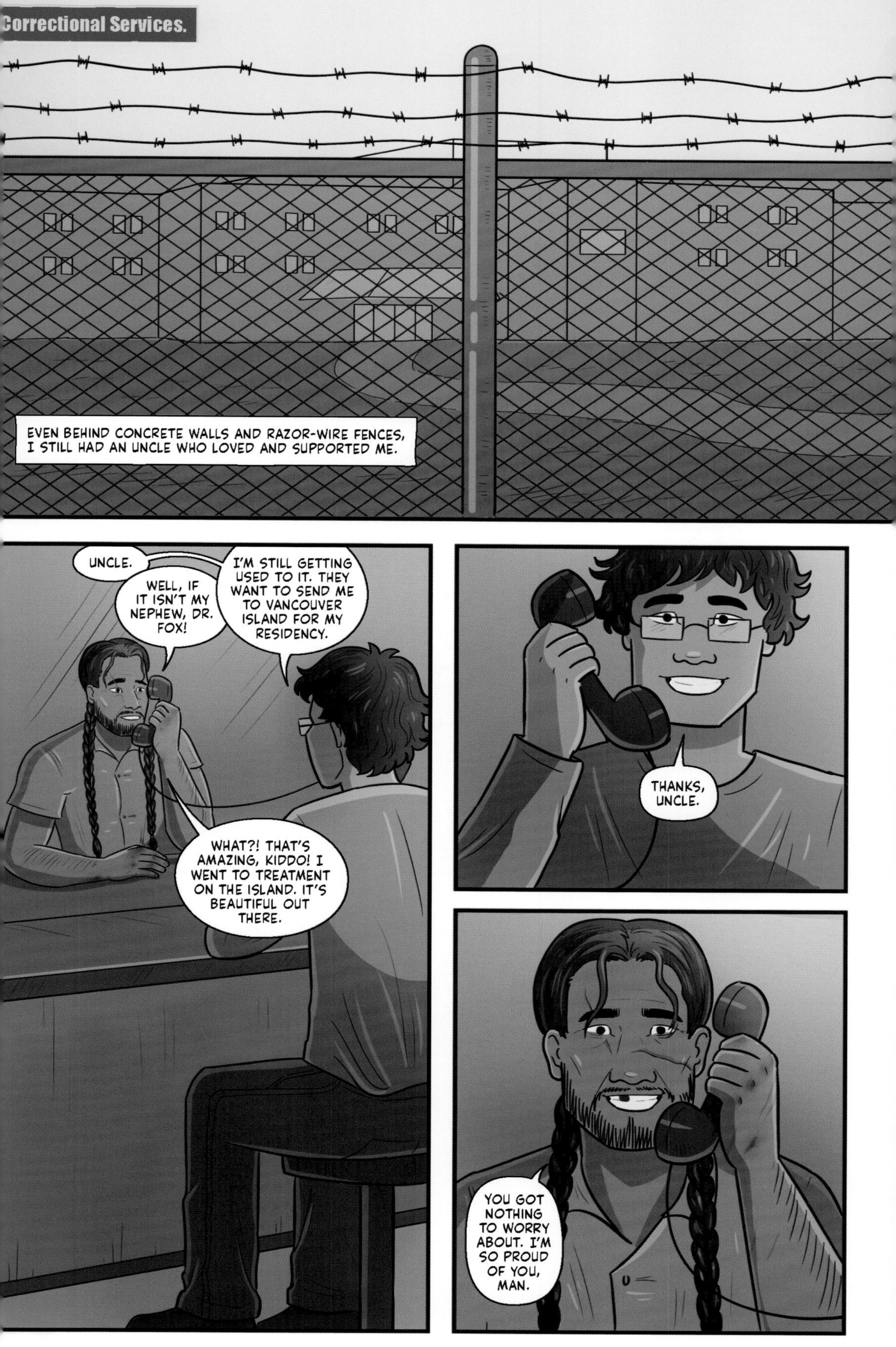
Correctional Services.
EVEN BEHIND CONCRETE WALLS AND RAZOR-WIRE FENCES, I STILL HAD AN UNCLE WHO LOVED AND SUPPORTED ME.
UNCLE.
WELL, IF IT ISN'T MY NEPHEW, DR. FOX!
I'M STILL GETTING USED TO IT. THEY WANT TO SEND ME TO VANCOUVER ISLAND FOR MY RESIDENCY.
WHAT?! THAT'S AMAZING, KIDDO! I WENT TO TREATMENT ON THE ISLAND. IT'S BEAUTIFUL OUT THERE.
THANKS, UNCLE.
YOU GOT NOTHING TO WORRY ABOUT. I'M SO PROUD OF YOU, MAN.

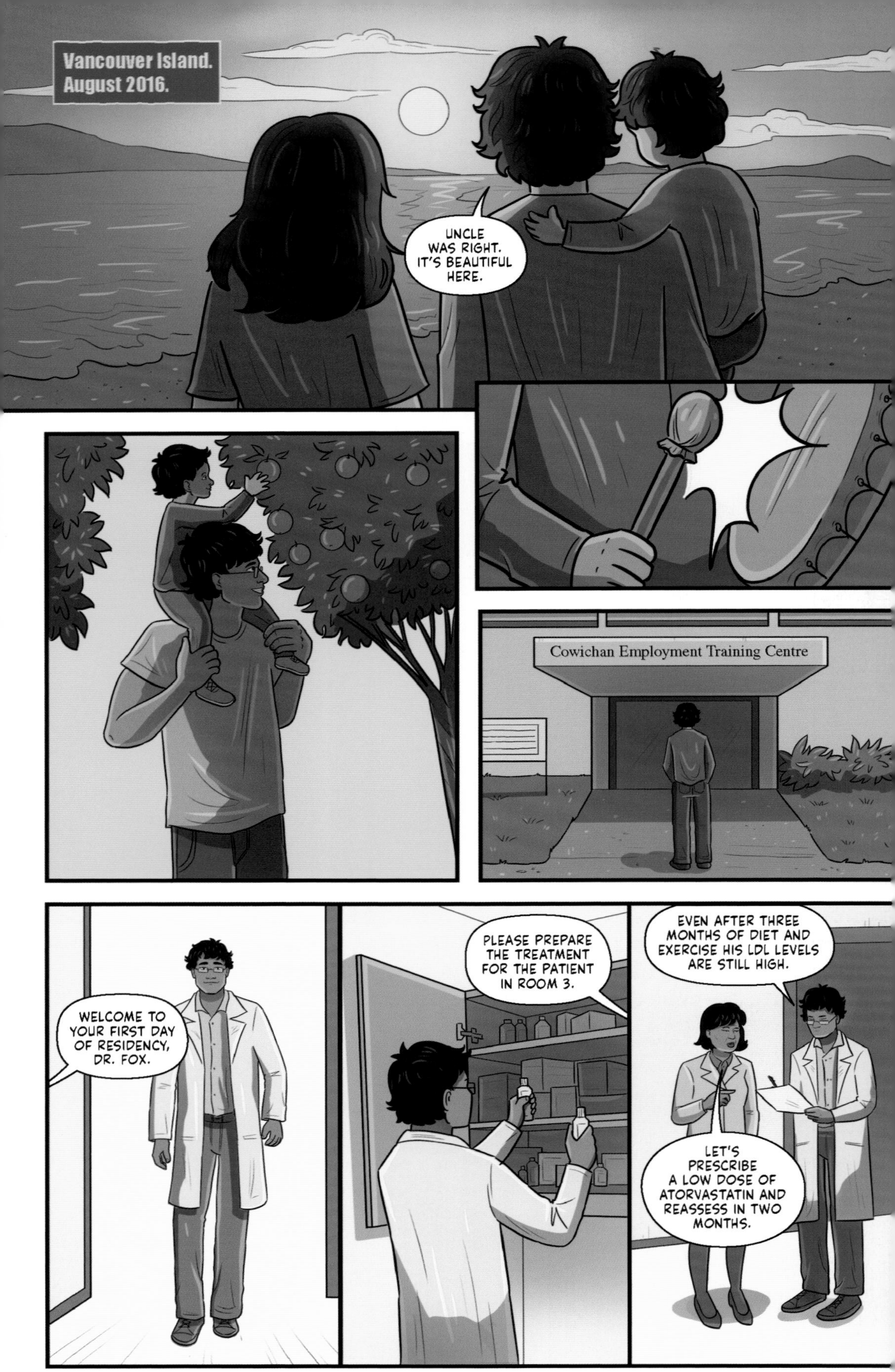
Vancouver Island.
August 2016.
UNCLE WAS RIGHT. IT'S BEAUTIFUL HERE.
Cowichan Employment Training Centre
WELCOME TO YOUR FIRST DAY OF RESIDENCY, DR. FOX.
PLEASE PREPARE THE TREATMENT FOR THE PATIENT IN ROOM 3.
EVEN AFTER THREE MONTHS OF DIET AND EXERCISE HIS LDL LEVELS ARE STILL HIGH.
LET'S PRESCRIBE A LOW DOSE OF ATORVASTATIN AND REASSESS IN TWO MONTHS.

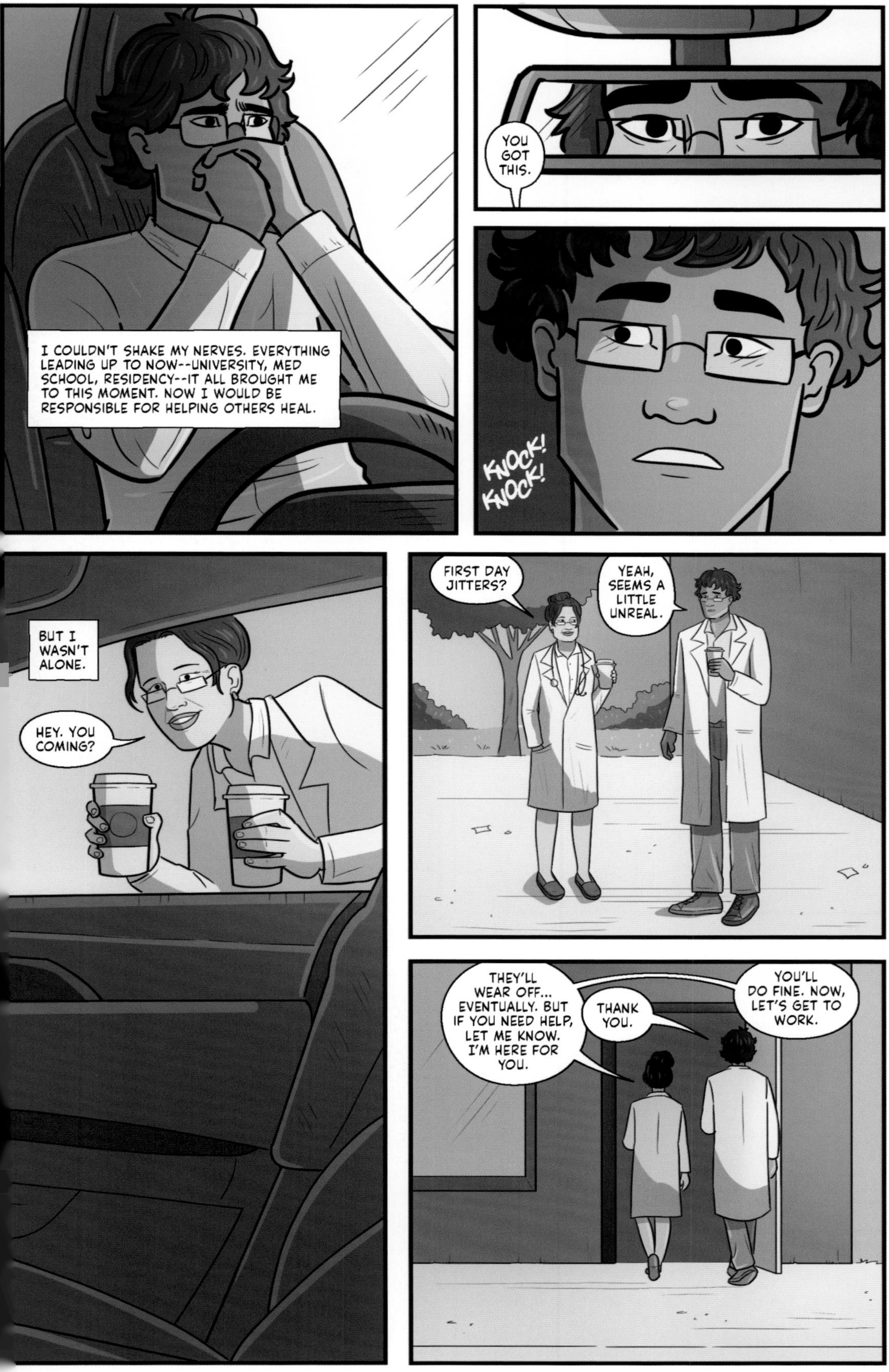
I COULDN'T SHAKE MY NERVES. EVERYTHING LEADING UP TO NOW--UNIVERSITY, MED SCHOOL, RESIDENCY--IT ALL BROUGHT ME TO THIS MOMENT. NOW I WOULD BE RESPONSIBLE FOR HELPING OTHERS HEAL.
YOU GOT THIS.
KNOCK! KNOCK!
BUT I WASN'T ALONE.
HEY. YOU COMING?
FIRST DAY JITTERS?
YEAH, SEEMS A LITTLE UNREAL.
THEY'LL WEAR OFF... EVENTUALLY. BUT IF YOU NEED HELP, LET ME KNOW. I'M HERE FOR YOU.
THANK YOU.
YOU'LL DO FINE. NOW, LET'S GET TO WORK.

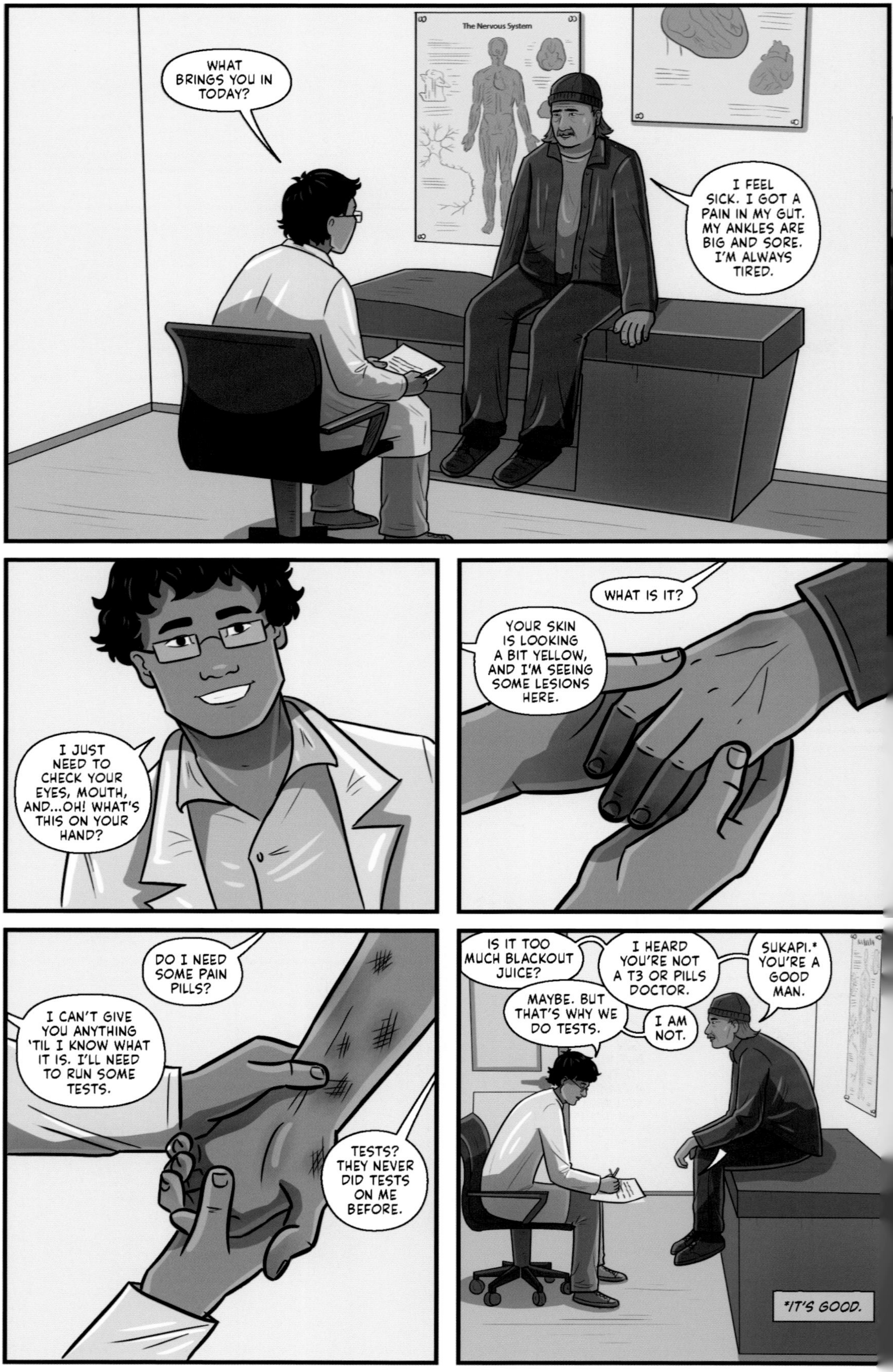
The Nervous System
WHAT BRINGS YOU IN TODAY?
I FEEL SICK. I GOT A PAIN IN MY GUT. MY ANKLES ARE BIG AND SORE. I'M ALWAYS TIRED.
I JUST NEED TO CHECK YOUR EYES, MOUTH, AND...OH! WHAT'S THIS ON YOUR HAND?
WHAT IS IT?
YOUR SKIN IS LOOKING A BIT YELLOW, AND I'M SEEING SOME LESIONS HERE.
DO I NEED SOME PAIN PILLS?
I CAN'T GIVE YOU ANYTHING 'TIL I KNOW WHAT IT IS. I'LL NEED TO RUN SOME TESTS.
TESTS? THEY NEVER DID TESTS ON ME BEFORE.
IS IT TOO MUCH BLACKOUT JUICE?
MAYBE. BUT THAT'S WHY WE DO TESTS.
I HEARD YOU'RE NOT A T3 OR PILLS DOCTOR.
I AM NOT.
SUKAPI.* YOU'RE A GOOD MAN.
*IT'S GOOD.

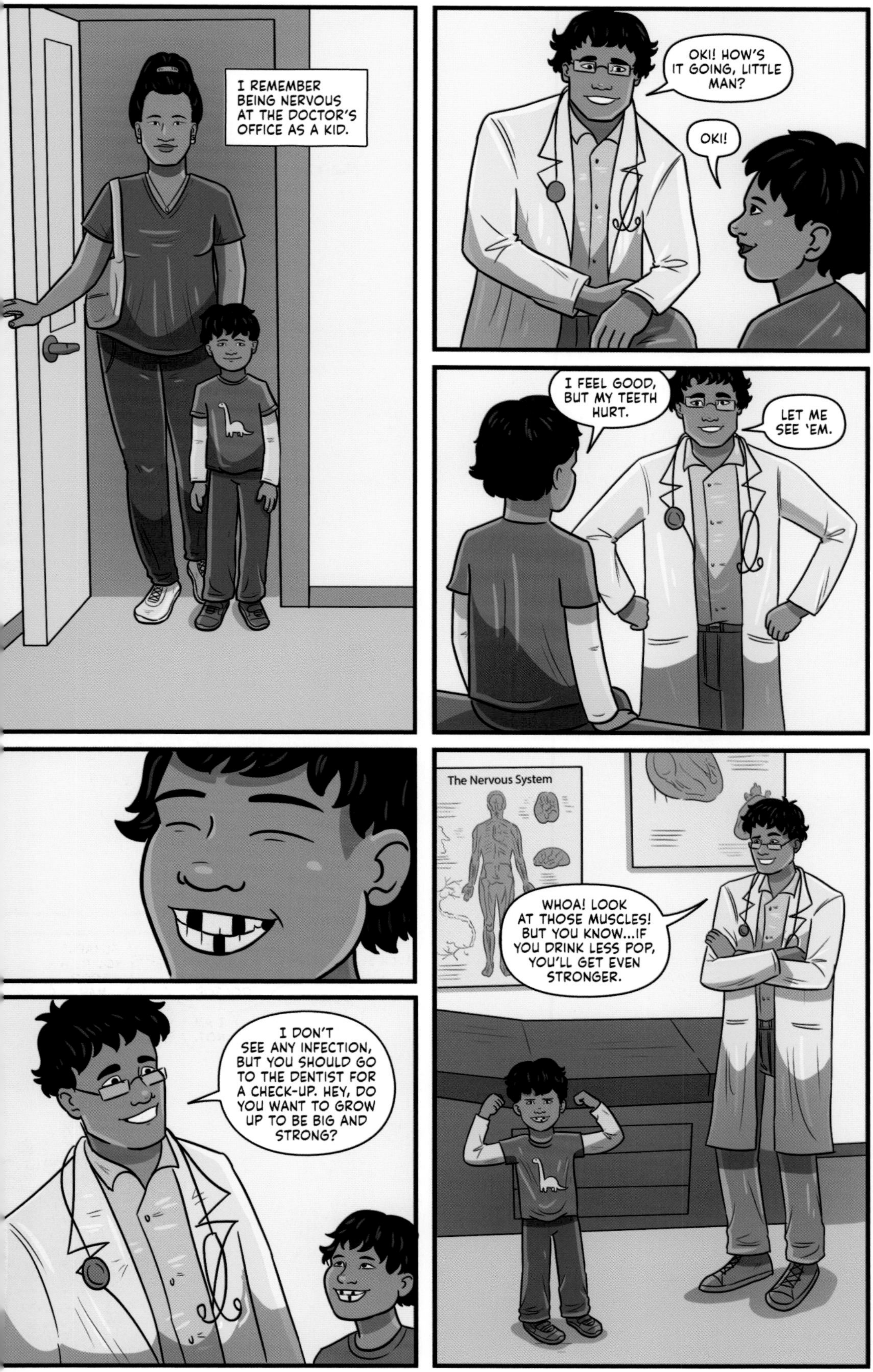
I REMEMBER BEING NERVOUS AT THE DOCTOR'S OFFICE AS A KID.
OKI! HOW'S IT GOING, LITTLE MAN?
OKI!
I FEEL GOOD, BUT MY TEETH HURT.
LET ME SEE 'EM.
I DON'T SEE ANY INFECTION, BUT YOU SHOULD GO TO THE DENTIST FOR A CHECK-UP. HEY, DO YOU WANT TO GROW UP TO BE BIG AND STRONG?
The Nervous System
WHOA! LOOK AT THOSE MUSCLES! BUT YOU KNOW...IF YOU DRINK LESS POP, YOU'LL GET EVEN STRONGER.

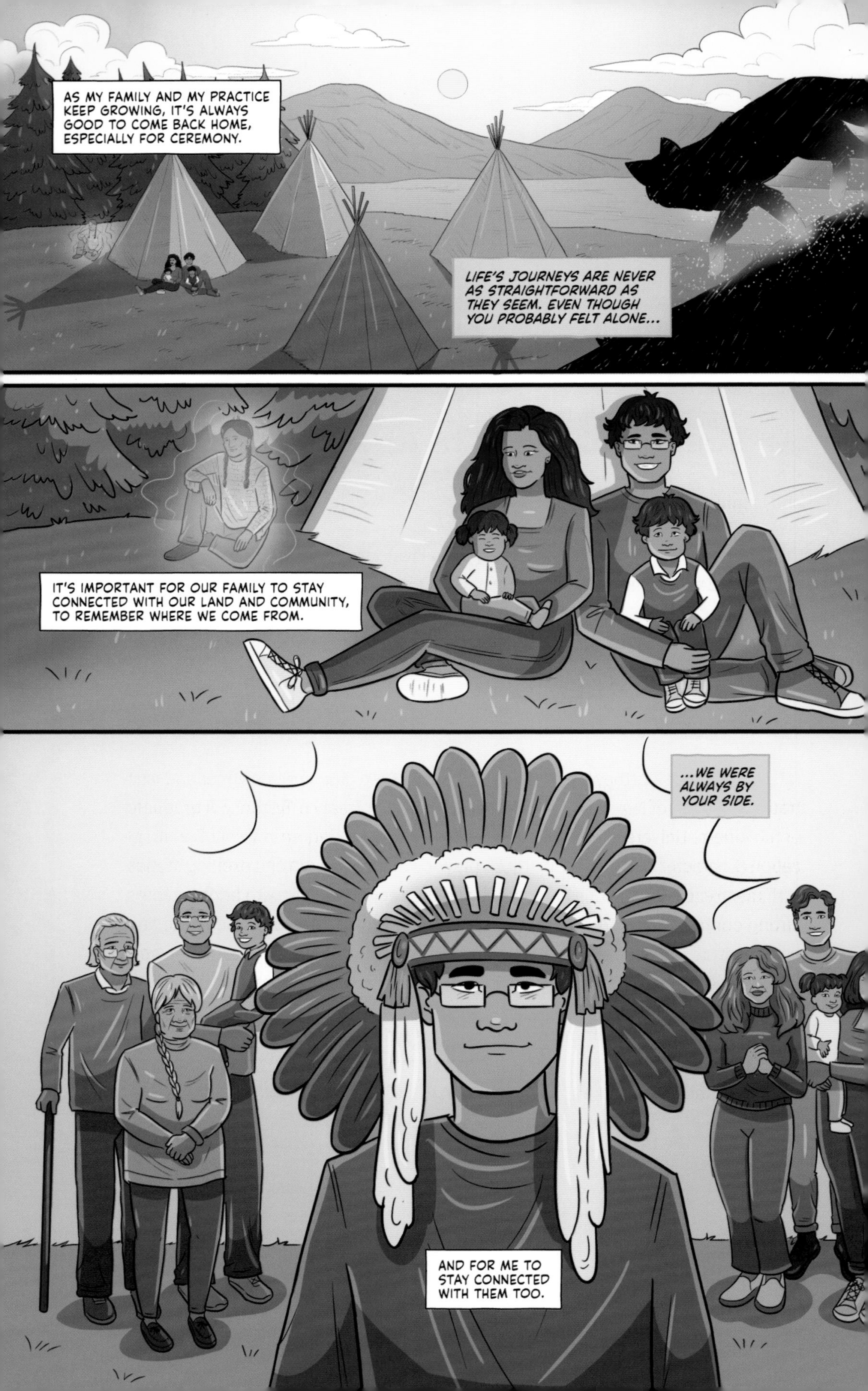
AS MY FAMILY AND MY PRACTICE KEEP GROWING, IT'S ALWAYS GOOD TO COME BACK HOME, ESPECIALLY FOR CEREMONY.
LIFE'S JOURNEYS ARE NEVER AS STRAIGHTFORWARD AS THEY SEEM. EVEN THOUGH YOU PROBABLY FELT ALONE...
IT'S IMPORTANT FOR OUR FAMILY TO STAY CONNECTED WITH OUR LAND AND COMMUNITY, TO REMEMBER WHERE WE COME FROM.
...WE WERE ALWAYS BY YOUR SIDE.
AND FOR ME TO STAY CONNECTED WITH THEM TOO.

GITZ CRAZYBOY (he/him/his) is a Siksikaitsitapi (Blackfoot) and Dene father and youth facilitator from Mohkínsstsisi (Calgary). Gitz's passion and purpose is helping, guiding, and most importantly, learning from the next generation, and he has held many positions within the youth education profession.

As an activist, Gitz is known for his leadership and participation in establishing the Bear Clan Patrol in Calgary, as well as organizing with the Idle No More movement. He has spent most of his life learning and living with different Indigenous Nations around the world. His travels have taken him to Germany, Ecuador, Guyana, Puerto Rico, and sacred spaces all over North America.

Currently Gitz resides in Calgary and is actively reconnecting with his Siksikaits-itapi roots. He believes the truth of who we are can be found in the beautiful things our ancestors carried—riddles, mysteries, ceremonies, songs, medicine, love, life, and laughter.

VERONIKA BARINOVA (she/her/hers) is an illustrator currently living in Calgary. She has a Bachelor in Visual Communication Design from the Alberta University of the Arts, and works primarily in digital media. Born in Moscow, Russia, Veronika is inspired by the 90s, occult fiction, and Slavic folk tales. Her work focuses on creating engaging characters and immersive worlds for readers, and her stories often have mystical or supernatural themes with a comedic undertone. Her work appears in *Giju's Gift* from the graphic novel series Adventures of the Pugulatmu'j.

AZBY WHITECALF (they/them/theirs) is a Plains Cree character designer and illus-trator based out of North Battleford, Saskatchewan in Treaty 6 Territory. A graduate of the Alberta University of the Arts, they hold a Bachelor Degree in Visual Communi-cation (Character Design). Their artistic practice focuses on fun and exciting stories with memorable and unique characters, and they enjoy working with bright colours, strong contrast, and fun shapes. Azby is passionate about creating accurate and positive representation of Indigenous Peoples and cultures, as well as exploring how to portray Indigenous Peoples in a way that celebrates multidimensional identities.

TOBEN RACICOT (he/him/his) is a comic book writer and letterer whose work has appeared in *Crown & Anchor*, *Pilgrim's Dirge*, *Beastlands*, *Sidequest*, and *Juniper*. He dreamt of being an aerospace engineer before failing high school physics. Now he studies role-playing games at the University of Waterloo.

HighWater Press gratefully acknowledges the financial support of the Government of Canada and Canada Council for the Arts as well as the Province of Manitoba through the Department of Sport, Culture, Heritage and Tourism and the Manitoba Book Publishing Tax Credit for our publishing activities.

Funded by the Government of Canada
Financé par le gouvernement du Canada

Canada

Canada Council   Conseil de arts
for the Arts   du Canada

HighWater Press is an imprint of Portage & Main Press
Printed and bound in Canada by Friesens
Design by Jennifer Lum
Cover art by Veronika Barinova
Colouring by Azby Whitecalf
Lettering by Toben Racicot

With thanks to the graphic arts student focus group from the Met Centre for Arts & Technology, Seven Oaks Met School, and Maples Met School (Winnipeg, MB) for their thoughtful feedback on the cover of this book.

This story is a work of fiction which is inspired, in part, by the lived experiences of Dr. Neill Fox. This story should not be considered to describe true and complete facts, details or events. Some of the names used throughout this story have been changed. The name of Dr. Tailfeathers has been used with their consent.

A big thank you to the Fox family, my mother, and the Creator of all things. Special thanks to Dr. Tailfeathers for being an inspiration, for protecting our people, and for being a guiding light. —**GC**

To my dad, who helped me fix the computer and tech I used to illustrate this graphic novel. —**VB**

For all of my relations who are struggling, may you find peace and strength with yourself and your family. —**AW**

Library and Archives Canada Cataloguing in Publication
Title: The rez doctor / Gitz Crazyboy, Veronika Barinova, Azby Whitecalf, Toben Racicot.
Names: Crazyboy, Gitz, author. | Barinova, Veronika, artist.
Description: Written by Gitz Crazyboy, artwork by Veronika Barinova, coloured by Azby Whitecalf, lettered by Toben Racicot.
Identifiers: Canadiana (print) 20230131700 | Canadiana (ebook) 20230131727 | ISBN 9781553799245 (softcover) | ISBN 9781553799252 (EPUB) | ISBN 9781553799269 (PDF) Subjects: LCGFT: Graphic novels.
Classification: LCC PN6733.C72 R49 2024 | DDC j741.5/971—dc23

27 26 25 24   1 2 3 4 5

This book was printed in North America by Friesens, the first FSC-certified printing company in Canada. With plants powered by hydroelectric and wind farms, the company is 100% employee-owned and is committed to minimizing its ecological footprint. It is printed on FSC-certified paper using vegetable-based inks and alcohol-free blanket wash.

MIX
Paper | Supporting
responsible forestry
FSC® C016245
www.fsc.org

HIGHWATER
PRESS
www.highwaterpress.com
Winnipeg, Manitoba
Treaty 1 Territory and homeland of the Métis Nation